SOULLESS

SAWYER BLACK

DAVID W. WRIGHT

STERLING & STONE

To YOU, the reader.
Thank you for taking a chance on us.
Thank you for your support.
Thank you for the emails.
Thank you for the reviews.
Thank you for reading and joining us on this road.

SOULLESS

SOULLESS

Chapter One

MICKAYLA COULDN'T BRING herself to pray anymore. How could she count her blessings after the doctor told her she was going to die? He put his hand on her knee. Shaking fingers. The contact of dry moth wings. She resisted the urge to jerk away.

Dr. Bailey cleared his throat. Shook his head. "This is *not* a death sentence."

He hadn't looked her in the eye a single time during her visit.

Surgery wasn't really an option. The cancer was everywhere. Neurofibrosarcomas. Tumors in the linings of her nerves. Radiating out from her spinal cord like a slow explosion.

She lowered the driver's window. Had some trouble with the crank. Such a simple motion, but unless she was looking, her arm just didn't seem to remember how to do it. Maybe she would swerve into oncoming traffic.

"You're such a drama queen."

Rose's voice sounded like it was in the passenger's seat next to her. Mickayla glanced over. Shrugged at the empty space before turning her attention back to the road. Nine in the morning on a Tuesday. Not much traffic on the back roads heading north out of Burg City. Away from the free clinics and orange barrels.

Across railroad tracks from the docks out east. Over bridges that crossed ocean water. Past private drives, and mailboxes that cost more than her apartment. Rich people secluding themselves back in the trees.

Real estate as old as the Choctaws they stole it from.

She reached for her cigarettes, but her numb fingers fumbled in the center console. It wasn't the long pack of the 100's. Not as long as the Lights either. Just the regular non-filter Smolders. Carl Iglesias called them cowboy killers. "Those are bad for you, kid," Rose said. Like she did every time Mickayla lit up.

Her hand finally figured it out, and she shook a cigarette free from the crinkling pack. Got it between her lips on the first try. Carl had given her the brass Zippo she used. That solid *clink* when she opened it. The pungent smell of the fluid. Oddly sweet. The heavy Catholic medallion glued to the case.

As a recovering Baptist, she hadn't known who St. Peregrine was. How she had laughed when she found out he was the patron saint of cancer victims. Oh, the irony. *Har har.*

She hadn't been inside a church since Rose died. Even now, with only weeks to live, she felt the same way about it as she had at nine years old. Just like the hospital was no place for sick people, the church was no place for sinners.

She and Rose said it at the same time. "Screw it."

Leaves scattered in her wake. Swirling into little tornadoes behind her. Pine trees and wet earth. The smell of a ruined childhood. At the fork in the road a mile past the Sloppy's that had been built with the county-mandated

Cape Cod architecture that swallowed the coastline, she was faced with her weekly choice. Left or right.

Left would take her deeper into the forest. Up into the hills. Old money and older sin. To the Viazo Grand Hotel where Amanda pushed her onto her next client. A lonely businessman. A gentleman in town for a convention. A politician looking for a safe taste of something that stretched his boundaries.

Or right …

Lake Winstead. The vacation spot for families with just enough money to look the part. Time-share cabins and community docks. The place of Mickayla's earliest memories. In her body as deeply as the cancer was.

Her fingers tightened on the wheel. Shoulders bunched up into tense knots. One day — today — maybe soon … she would whip that little car down through the gap on the right. Over the hill that always made her stomach fly up into her throat. Winding her way through walnut trees. Feeling the seeds smoosh under the tires.

She would park. Leave her cigarettes inside the car. Walk to the little dock at the edge of the beach. The one hidden by the hanging brambles. Out to the end where the railing stopped. She would sit with her feet dangling over the edge, barely scraping the swells of the lake's surface.

She would lean back and tip her head up. Breathe the lake through her nose.

Footsteps behind her. Bare feet scraping along smooth planks. She would know the gait as she knew her own.

Rose.

Her sister's hand would fall on her shoulder, and they would be together again. Twenty years after she felt those little fingers slip from her cold grasp. The sting of the waves on her own face as she fell in after her. Rose's terrified eyes as they rushed into the darkness, pulled by a wave rolling back into the dark water.

If only she could have held on.

Like always, Mickayla took the left fork, and her dead twin sighed in her ear. "One of these days, kid."

The wind pulled the smoke through the open window. Stoked the ember at the end of the cigarette. She was already halfway through the pack. Five in a row sitting outside the doctor's office.

A warped park bench under a shedding maple. She wondered what the bark would feel like under her fingers. It seemed her body had forgotten what touch was like.

Fine details of texture. Temperature. Pain. A decline she had barely noticed, until one day she looked down at the blood coming from a slash in the webbing between her thumb and forefinger. Cutting coupons with a monstrous set of kitchen scissors, and she hadn't even felt it.

She had blinked in disbelief. Set the scissors down and made fists. Pressed her fingertips harder and harder into her palms. Until her forearms shook, and eight little half-moon bruises had formed.

She looked at her hands like they belonged to someone else. There was weight. Awareness. But nothing else. She lit a cigarette. Took a long drag to get it hot. Stubbed it out on the back of her hand with a wince of anticipation.

The healing scar looked like a giant freckle. It stretched into an oval when she closed her fist, but like the day she first made it, she still didn't feel it.

Her decline had been swift — and inevitable. Her feet had turned into blocks of wood. Her hands were fumbling mittens. She couldn't feel the cigarette between her lips, and if she didn't pay attention, she dribbled coffee down her chin.

The discovery was two weeks ago. She probably had two weeks left. For once, Rose had nothing to say.

Mickayla flicked the cigarette out the window a few yards before her turn. She would rather litter on the road than in the parking lot of the Viazo Grand.

It was an old and beautiful property, but it wasn't respect that made her want to keep it clean. It was the dragon. The stylized worm hanging above the doors. Set into the tile of the entryway. Painted on all the ceilings. Swooping wings and fiery breath. She could feel it watching her, and even though she never once threw a butt on the ground where it could see her, she felt its judgement just the same.

"You're weird," Rose whispered.

Mickayla shrugged. Steered away from the front entrance. Around back where the rest of the help went inside — out of sight of the *real* money. She'd gone through the front doors plenty of times, but always on the arm of somebody paying her way.

On *her* nights, the concierge had always been the same. Peterson, with his Cockney affectations and his insufferable corporate loyalty. To his credit, he had always pretended not to know her. To keep up the client's expectations, or maybe because he truly couldn't be bothered to remember her name.

It didn't matter now. Soon, she'd be dead, and he wouldn't have to bother.

She parked next to Amanda's Lincoln. Rose's sigh sounded like it was coming up the side. Like she had gotten out before the car had stopped and was walking up to open Mickayla's door for her. "What did I say earlier about drama queens?"

Mickayla ignored her. Reached behind the passenger seat to snatch her purse off the floor. She dug in for the small bottle of mouthwash. Almost dropped it trying to compress the childproof cap.

Swished and swirled, and only realized her mistake when she heard Rose's laughter.

The dragon would see if she spit it out on the ground, so she swallowed with a sneer. Gasped fresh air past burning gums.

Amanda rarely called her for a job during the week, and never this early in the day. And admitting she didn't really feel like having sex with a stranger would prompt Amanda to look at her with confusion to ask, "Do you ever?"

Mickayla shook her head with a chuckle. Winced when the door hinge creaked like bending metal. Looked around in sheepish apology, but nobody was watching. Except for the Viazo Grand mascot.

"I wonder what his name is?" Rose asked.

Mickayla shrugged as she closed her door. "Chester?"

"He doesn't look like a Chester."

"Then what's he look like?"

"I don't know. Something old and dangerous. Like Brad."

The door's closing groan cut off when it slammed shut, and Mickayla smoothed the front of her skirt. She couldn't feel them, but she knew her palms were clammy.

"I doubt if it's Brad," she said, and she could almost feel her sister's hair brush her face as Rose shook her head.

"You never know."

There were no trucks or trailers yet. No deliveries or pickups. The click of her heels echoed back from the sloped docks. Rang off the featureless metal doors.

She walked past modern architecture that gave way to brick and plaster. Wood and iron. Almost like stepping back in time.

Even the sound of her shoes sounded different. More subdued. Like they were coming from somebody following her.

Angular hedges positioned to hide the rear of the hotel from view of the arriving guests from the road, and as she stepped into a path of smooth stones sunk into a carpet of moss, the air cooled.

She only ever saw working girls like her on this path. Thin and gorgeous, with the genetics to keep them that way in spite of their lifestyles. Chain-smoking, pill-popping alcoholics mostly. Running from trouble. *Toward* trouble.

Or the trouble somebody *else* was running away from.

She passed a stone bench that nobody ever sat on. Passed a fountain nobody wished at.

Unlike the rest of the hotel, there were no electronic locks on the door she approached. This one opened with an old brass key.

It made her feel special. Like she was part of some secret society, even though she couldn't match the name to the face of a single girl in her little club. They were all part of the oldest profession in the world — next to carpentry — and she only knew them by sight. The smell of their perfume under the stale cigarette smoke. The sound of their walk.

Amanda often referred to them by name. "Oh, Sara will have to come in this Thursday night. Senator McCallister likes darker skin."

Even with that clue, Mickayla couldn't place her. She wondered if the others felt the same way about her. "Of course they do," Rose said.

The key slipped inside without resistance, and she nodded in agreement as the lock clicked over. "You're probably right."

Rose was almost always right.

A small tiled entryway. A set of ornate chairs along the right side. Wrought-iron hooks set into mahogany panels along the left. Gold and red was the palate of the Viazo Grand.

A wide doorway with stained glass transom and side-lights. And that damn dragon painted on a domed ceiling so high, it seemed to defy the logic of construction.

Mickayla passed into the main hallway. Wide and tall, its deep scarlet carpet led to a staircase. The railing swept to either side to join a set of railings on the above floor. Each one overlooking the entry. It was a miniature version of the main entrance on the other side of the hotel.

It felt like a mile away through a maze of hallways, and Mickayla wondered just how big the entire place was. One day, she would have to find out.

Her toe caught on the first step, and she paused to recover her balance. Her knuckles popped when she grabbed the railing, and she closed her eyes. There would be no *one day*.

Soon, there would be no more days at all.

"Give me a break," Rose said.

Mickayla shrugged. Squared her shoulders and climbed the stairs. To the door centered at the top. Amanda was expecting her so she didn't bother knocking.

Her back was to the door. Shoulders hunched and head down. A graceful spin brought her hands out like she was trying to take flight. Shocked face like she had been caught doing something wicked.

Amanda Dior looked like flesh in stone. Carved from perfect blocks of creamy marble. Visible veins tracing a green highway under pale skin. Eyes that glittered like silver. Platinum hair in funky spikes.

The lithe body of a dancer and the filthy mouth of a

construction worker. Mickayla liked her, but Rose *adored* her.

"Where have you been?" Her pronunciation was harshly proper. Clipped and pointed like the sharp edge of broken dinnerware. Mickayla had never been able to place her accent. Told herself *British* and let it go. "Do you have a cigarette?"

Mickayla stumbled as she closed the door behind her. She had never seen Amanda smoke. "What?"

Amanda put her hands on her hips and leaned forward. "Do you have a cigarette? Please."

Mickayla set her purse on the desk. "I was at the doctor's office."

"Yes?" Amanda sounded impatient. Like someone who wasn't listening.

The Smolders had worked their way under a pack of tissues. Like they were running away from her fingers. She pulled them out and shook one free. Amanda snatched it out of the pack before Mickayla could even extend her arm.

Amanda stared at her hand as it went back inside for the lighter. "Go ahead," she said. "I don't want to smoke alone."

It wasn't until she had finished lighting Amanda's cigarette that she realized she had been given permission to smoke too. Amanda continued to watch through a haze of smoke, and Mickayla kept her head down.

That dragon was on the ceiling of the office too. Crimson paint and gold leaf twining through the coffers. There was no way to avoid its gaze.

"You're out of control," Rose said through a giggle.

"Where were you?" Amanda asked.

Mickayla blew smoke from her nose. "Getting my diagnosis."

Amanda's hands trembled as she lifted the cigarette back to her lips, and Mickayla realized that even though the other woman's eyes seemed to be staring right at her, they weren't seeing her. They were looking at someone far away.

Their ashes grew in silence until Amanda caught her breath. Looked down at her cigarette. Back up to Mickayla's face. "I'm sorry, darling. What did you say?"

"It was just a little car trouble."

"I told you to get something better than that rusting shit box you love so much."

An empty candy dish became an ashtray as Mickayla stubbed her cigarette out. "Don't ask," Rose whispered.

Mickayla sighed. "Amanda, what is it?"

The ash broke from Amanda's cigarette. Exploded into a dusty puff on the tip of her cream-colored high heels. "You have a client in Room Three. Asked for you by name. This man …"

She brought the cigarette up. Noticed it had gone out. Lowered her hand in disappointment.

Mickayla slid the strap of her purse up on her shoulder. "What about this man?"

"He said he would be your last."

Rose groaned. "Told you not to ask."

Chapter Two

MICKAYLA HAD BEEN lucky her entire life. At least, that's what everybody told her.

All the way back to that summer at the lake. Sure, her twin sister was dead, but at least she had survived. Safe in the arms of loving parents.

Until they had gotten divorced a year later.

Grief, guilt, and blame, but at least it wasn't aimed at her. Until it was.

"Why did he leave, Mama?"

Her mother had paused with the wine bottle poised over the rim of the stained glass. "Because you couldn't hold on. Just a *little* bit longer."

The sound of the glass filling covered up Mickayla's gasp of shock and pain. She left the room without another word. Crawled under the blankets. Left Lamby outside on the cold floor.

The little stuffed sheep. Worn and dirty. Mickayla never picked her up again, because when she pressed her face into the pillow to silence her screams, she felt the bed rock under the weight of somebody sitting beside her.

She threw the blankets off and spread her arms to fall into the embrace of her mother. Ready to breathe in the rotten smell of the wine, but nobody was there.

Lamby looked up at her from the floor. Her floppy head twisted sideways over her little flower-print dress.

A warm arm slid across the back of her neck, and she froze. The smell of wet earth and duckweed drifted by, and the arm tightened against her. Cold fingers caressed her upper arm.

"You held on as long as you could," Rose said.

Mickayla cried for hours. Rose stroked her hair. The room grew dark, and it was well after her bedtime when her mother threw the door open to lean against the jamb with the light behind her making her edges look like she was on fire.

"The hell you crying about now?"

Lucky for Mickayla, she didn't say anything about Rose, and after that night, everybody told her mother how lucky she was that her daughter was adjusting so well.

Her mother died two years later when she aspirated her own vomit after her fourth bottle of wine in less than two hours. Even then, Rose had known just what to say.

"Drowning sucks, but at least I did it like a normal person."

She had been standing at the edge of the bed. Looking down at her mother's body. Cordless phone dangled from her fingers. A fireman scooped her up, but when she cackled at Rose's joke, he stumbled. Almost dropped her, and it made her laugh harder.

She nearly peed herself.

At least she was lucky enough to have another parent who could take her in.

She was more of a ghost in that man's house than Rose

was. He barely spoke to her — never looked at her — but at least he bought her food. Gave her money for clothes.

A couple different stepmothers there to teach a few important points of hygiene. Delores was the best one. Tall and blonde, and they had been mistaken for mother and daughter many times. But she had left when her father had cheated on her with Ramona.

Short and thick with dark hair, she acted like getting her father's attention was a competition, so Mickayla let her win.

School was a breeze. It just came so easy for her. How lucky …

Not many friends since she had Rose, but she was still popular. Never *in* the clique but still accepted. Fortunate.

One day when she jumped into Johnny Denton's pool with her clothes on, she noticed she couldn't hear Rose's voice over the sound of the water rushing past her ears.

She blew her air out and crossed her legs. Settled to the bottom and waited for the light to dim. Closed her eyes. Smiled to herself before taking a deep breath.

Luckily, Johnny's father dove in and pulled her out.

She woke up in the hospital three days later. Rose wouldn't talk to her, but a small woman with a clipboard over her chest was more than happy to fill the void.

"Let's talk about your sister," she said, and she lifted a gold pen to the paper on the clipboard and waited for Mickayla to tell her everything.

She turned eighteen the next summer. Stopped going to therapy but kept the valium prescription. Dr. Legane had been pleased with her progress, and was happy to let her give it a go by herself. Even Rose thought it was premature.

Ramona sat her down. Handed her an envelope. "Your

father believes he has done right by you. You're lucky he's a good man."

Ten thousand dollars and a list of apartment buildings south of Burg City. Fifteen hundred dollars of it went to a Subaru Wagon with rust on the fenders, but the interior was perfect, and the engine was smooth and quiet.

Ramona's cousin worked at a used car lot out in East Side almost underneath the J. Moses East Bridge, and he assured her over and over that she had gotten a *great fucking* deal. That car was a lucky find.

The first apartment she looked at was taken. A nice place next to the docks. Not in the ghetto, but ghetto-adja- cent. Close enough to the nightlife to make the price out of her budget, but far enough away from crime to make it reasonably safe for a young woman on her own.

Especially a woman blessed with good looks. Ramona had told her there would plenty of men willing to pay for a night in her bed. Sneered in disgust when she said how nice it must be to never have to put in any effort.

The apartment manager called her that first night. Manny Greeco. He asked her to dinner, and over the first round of drinks, he made it clear how she might be able to get on the list for the next opening.

He was her father's age. Handsome in a *trying too hard* kind of way. He was clean, and his breath smelled like cinnamon. She knew she could do worse, and *had* done worse before. Johnny Denton had been young and hard, but insecure and inexperienced.

Fumbling and resentful of her impatience, and the only thing she got out of it was an admiring glance from Peggy Stewart, and the jealous glare of Liz Mansfield, Johnny's ex-girlfriend.

She stayed with Manny for a week. He came home happy to see her. Told her she was wearing him out.

An apartment came open, and true to his word, she went to the front of the list. Two days later, she was supposed to move in, but she stayed in Manny's bed.

He had a heart attack moving a dishwasher up to the fifth floor, and the *new* manager wanted to stay offsite. Asked her if she wanted to take over Manny's lease.

He had no family. Few friends. He was a dirtbag. A sleaze that used his power to get a girl in his bed, and she was suddenly in possession of the lease to an apartment she couldn't afford.

Worn furniture. Huge stereo with a vintage record collection. Late night knocks on the door from residents wanting their AC fixed.

She donated his clothes to Goodwill and took a close look at her bank account. If she drank most of her diet, eating what Manny had left behind in the cabinets, she'd have about six months. Why not make them good ones?

She took over Manny's lease, and the apartment he had promised her went to a Jewish shut-in who did nothing but look at the dirty water slapping against the algae-stained pylons next to the waterfront.

Rose told her she could be a stripper. "*They* made a lot of money, right? Always putting themselves through medical school?"

She found herself at Hector's Basement, and that's where she met Carl Iglesias. The first time she *really* felt lucky. The huge Mexican bouncer stopped her at the front door. Gave her a look that said, "We both know you ain't twenty-one."

His face looked like scorched oatmeal, but his eyes were sad, and his smile was beautiful and open and honest. His voice softened when he talked to her, and she asked if she could just stick around and talk.

His eyebrows rose, and those perfect teeth flashed. "With me?"

There was nobody in line to get in. Just the muted sound of the music from the stage. The water against the pier.

She pulled her cigarettes out and shook loose a Smolders non-filter, and he threw back his head and laughed. "Damn girl, you smoke like a man."

She offered him one, and he took it with a shake of his head. She lit it for him with the tiny Bic she had found on Manny's nightstand.

She sat by his side, and when the club closed down, and when the owner shook Carl's hand and locked the front door, they still sat there. Finished the rest of the pack, then she took him to her new apartment.

Told him how she got it as she pulled him into the bedroom. He had the look of a man who couldn't believe what he was seeing. A magic trick that defied all reason and logic. "You ain't lucky," he said. "*I* am."

They took her valium and drank Manny's cheap scotch, and Carl undressed her like he was afraid she would shatter.

His body was powerful. His long black hair as smooth as silk. The ends smelled like smoke, but his scalp smelled like coconut. His big hands were gentle. Rough skin made softer by his tentative touch.

It felt like she deserved it. Like she had been waiting for it, and if it hadn't been for Rose's soft whisper, she would have thanked God. But that would have been too much praying.

She cried into his shoulder, and he held her to him. Spoke Spanish in her ear in a rumbling whisper.

They got out of bed, and he dug through Manny's kitchen. Exclaimed in surprise as he pulled ingredients out of the pantry cabinets next to the fridge. Fried them up some homemade tortillas. Cussed and laughed as the popping oil spit at him until he tied a towel around his waist.

He filled the tortillas with eggs, and they ate them with the rest of the scotch. He asked her what she was going to do, and she shrugged.

"That's a good question," Rose had said.

Carl told her he had to get home to his dog — a troubled pit bull named Lita — but he had an idea. He was gonna introduce her to somebody. A chick that worked at the Viazo Grand. One that sent her girls down this way for the easy pickings.

"We got a understanding," he'd said.

Mickayla went to sleep with the sun coming up, and for once didn't dream of cold water. Sinking down into the cold depths. Her hand open in front of her, but no fingers coming to grab it.

Later that week, Carl had introduced her to Amanda Dior.

The next week Amanda had introduced her to Walt Prescott, a balding businessman with a paunch and double chins. He wanted a quiet evening dinner with a young woman, and when he saw her, his face opened in shock.

She had never felt more beautiful.

Room Number Three to the left at the top of the stairs. A bottle of wine and four valiums later, and it was over barely before it had begun. He spent an hour in her arms afterward. Shaking his head and thanking her.

That night paid for an entire month's rent.

How lucky for her.

After three months, she got a better apartment. Moved Manny's stereo and record collection to the top floor.

SAWYER BLACK & DAVID W. WRIGHT

Bought new furniture. New clothes. Carl got her valium. The Viazo Grand got her wine.

What a life to lead, and all she had to do was let her sister die.

The purse slid from her shoulder to catch on the crook of her elbow. She dropped it back on Amanda's desk. Lit another cigarette and blew the smoke up at the ceiling. "Well, lucky me," she said.

Amanda took the lit cigarette from her finger. "Darling, you don't know what you're saying. Let me explain—"

Mickayla pointed a fresh cigarette at the dragon painted above them. "You happen to know his name?"

Amanda shook her head in confusion. "Arktis."

Mickayla nodded before lighting the cigarette. "What is that, Latin?"

Amanda looked down with a frown. "Much older than that."

"You know what it means?"

"The one who watches."

Rose laughed, and it sounded like she clapped her hands in glee. "Ha! Figures ... the watcher."

Amanda waved smoke from her face. "I don't see why this is funny. I need to tell you something." She swallowed and shook her head. Tears pooled in the inside corners of her eyes.

Mickayla smiled. "You are *so* pretty. Like from another world."

Amanda drew back. "Thank you. But darling—"

"Has it cost you anything?"

Rose snorted in her ear. "Kind of question is that?"

Amanda turned away to lean against her desk. "You have no idea."

Mickayla sighed. "I only have a couple weeks to live. This guy was gonna be my last one anyway."

She left her purse but kept the cigarette. Turned without looking back. "You don't understand ..." Amanda's voice trailed off, and she didn't try to stop Mickayla from leaving the office.

Lucky her.

The door closing behind her sounded like every door had slammed at the same time. Echoes tumbling into the rounded plaster of the vaulted ceiling.

Mickayla looked up at the dragon. Suspended in perpetual flight above her. Now that she knew his name, she didn't feel so small. "You suppose she thinks I'm a weirdo?"

Arktis didn't answer. He just watched her through the rising cloud of cigarette smoke.

"What other people think of you is none of your business," Rose said. "Just assume they don't like you and get on with it. Things are easier that way."

Mickayla smiled and reached up to pick off a bit of tobacco stuck to her tongue. She turned toward Room Number Three. That significant door. The one that started this phase of her life.

Appropriate that it would be the one where her life ended.

Rose growled. "You didn't let Amanda finish. You don't know what's gonna happen in that room."

"Maybe not, but I know how everything else ends."

"I'm not dumber than you, Mickayla. Just deader."

"Then *you* know how it ends too."

Before Rose could answer, she knocked on the door. More echoes. Another drag from her Smolder non-filter.

Come in.

She didn't hear the voice. The words just appeared in her awareness. She lifted her hand to the doorknob, but Rose brought her up short. "Bullshit."

"What is?"

"I heard a voice. You trying to tell me you didn't?"

Mickayla shook her head. She couldn't really remember. The knob turned under her fingers. She snatched her hand away and took a step back.

The door swung open, but there was nobody on the other side. At the end of its swing, it hit the wall. Nowhere for anyone to hide.

"Fuck this," Rose whispered.

It was dark. Every light was out. The curtains drawn. Mickayla knew the room. She had been in it often enough.

The thick red and gold carpet continued throughout. A sitting area with antique chairs to match the ones at the bottom of the stairs. Marble tables and counters. Borderless mirrors.

The bathroom was 1940's luxury. Ceilings that seemed higher than the roof of the hotel. Heavy wallpaper. Silk and gold.

The bed was enormous. Piled high with pillows, and the wooden joints of the walnut frame were so tight, they would never squeak, no matter how much force they were subjected to.

It was the nicest place she had ever been.

"Seriously," Rose said. "Let's just fuck off."

Mickayla stepped into the room the same way she had walked through her whole life. Without worry. Not a care in the world.

Whatever was on the other side of the doorway couldn't compare to watching her sister's mouth fill with dirty water.

The door closed behind her with a near-silent *click*. A push of air at her back.

A man spoke. "I waited a long time for you."

It was as if the voice came from all around her. Like

she stood in the center of an orchestra. The music of his words were a physical pressure against her, but the meaning of his speech floated into her consciousness like they were placed there.

She thought them instead of hearing them.

"I told you to run," Rose said.

Mickayla opened her eyes to the limit. Faint light from around the edges of the heavy drapes swelled as her vision adjusted. She swallowed before answering. "I came as soon as I was able."

"Thousands of years." His words were just the echo of meaning. Like a door slamming at the top of the stairs.

"Oh, fuck *this*," Rose said.

Mickayla held her hand out and walked toward the bar. "Where are you?"

"Your thread wound through the cloth of the world before the disciples ever gathered at the hem of His robe."

"I know what it is," Rose said. "You're dying. Dr. Bailey was wrong. It's happening now."

Mickayla's hand found the crystal lamp at the end of the bar. Its shade rattled as she reached under it to find the chain. "What disciples?" she asked.

His sigh sounded like a waterfall pouring over a mountain a thousand miles away. "It was woven into many. In and around so much sin."

"Yep," Rose said. "It hit your brain and now you're seeing things. *Hearing* things."

Mickayla finally got the gold chain between numb fingers. Pulled it down hard enough to tilt it toward the edge of the counter. She caught it as the bulb flared to life, and the light hit her right in the face.

She looked away as she righted the lamp. Lifting her hand and cracking one eye open to make sure it was stable.

A bright spot formed in front of her eyes as she turned

to look deeper into the room. She hissed in pain when the cigarette burned into the knuckles of her other hand. She dropped it out of reflex, and the coal flared as it fell.

It hit the carpet in a cascade of sparks, and she jumped back, only to growl and hop back forward. She stomped out the glow and wondered if Arktis was watching.

Peterson would have a shit fit when he found out she had burned the carpet.

"Are you fucking kidding me?" Rose shouted.

Her words overlapped those of the voice in the room. "And the thread of your life led me here."

Mickayla looked up from under her brows. He was on the bed. Pillows and blankets all around him.

"Maybe that's all him," Rose said.

Mickayla shook her head. Slid the lamp to the other end of the bar as she walked toward the bed.

It *was* all him.

He was a massive man. The wrinkled sheet was pulled to his waist, and his feet stuck out the bottom. He was much larger than Carl. Maybe the biggest man she had ever seen. Glistening skin the color of oiled oak. Veins in sharp relief over striated muscles. Dark hair and beard sweeping away from a smooth face.

"He's beautiful," Rose said.

Mickayla nodded, then she froze. Tilted her head. Focused on his arm.

Above the bulge of his biceps was a rubber tube. Knotted but loose. In the hollow of his elbow was a needle. Hanging from the skin, it bobbed with his heartbeat.

"I knew it," Rose said.

The man looked down to follow her gaze. He smiled. "I must first know the sin if I am to forgive it."

His mouth hadn't moved, but Mickayla heard the words as before. Rose was right. The cancer had reached her brain sooner than expected, and now she was going to die.

"Not today, child," he said.

He sat up and lifted his other hand. In his fist hung a scrap of cloth. Dirty and ragged. "This is all that's left of His robe. The one He wore in Bethsaida. It healed a blind man at the mere touch of his finger against the trailing hem."

"I have to get out of here," Mickayla said.

Rose sighed. It sounded like she crossed her arms. "Too late."

The man threw the sheet aside, and his erection bounced up from the shadow. Mickayla spun to leave, but his voice commanded her. "Be still."

Her feet were rooted. her hands were fists pressing into her thighs. Her teeth clenched together.

She felt the vibration of his weight settling on the floor. "Every thread I chased through the fabric of creation caused another thread to loosen in the fabric of this cloth. But I no longer fret, for I have found you."

The floor shuddered. The wooden bed frame groaned. Mickayla wanted to know what he was doing, but she couldn't look. "He's standing on the bed," Rose said.

"His power was His divine right," the man said. His voice rolled against her back like the incoming tide. "It was His gift to Man. It entered everything it touched. Lived on in the things He held dear. Passed from contact to soul, but never possessed, for there was no mortal with the ability to hold it as dearly as He had."

Mickayla didn't want to hear anymore. She just wanted a drink. A valium. A cigarette. An open fucking door.

"But there was one," he continued. "One that would have the connection to His divine light. A void reached by a thread of love. A sister woven into her story — held by the stitches of His touch."

A sister? Mickayla shook her head. "What?" Rose said. "You really think I'm just a ghost?"

"A sister held inside her own soul."

"… just a figment of your imagination?"

"Touched by the son of God, but held away from His love."

"… some hallucination?"

"Nay, she is not a thought, but a reality. And her sister is a being that will hold the healing of His hand in her own heart, and she will restore the world."

"Should have left when you had the chance," Rose said.

"Raise your eyes, child. Behold!"

Mickayla's body betrayed her. It turned without her will. In *spite* of her desire to run screaming. She looked up, and her neck burned with her efforts to look away.

The man stood in the center of the bed with his arms outstretched. The rubber tubing on his arm popped off with a snap of elastic. The needle fell out, followed by a rush of black blood. It dripped in spreading splotches on the stark white sheets.

His body was perfection, and she caught her breath. The room brightened to reveal every inch of skin, and she realized the light was coming from *him*.

His chest expanded, and the mattress decompressed as he rose into the air. His head brushed the ceiling, and he looked down at her with a gentle smile. "I have come to find the sins of one sinner in particular. The great serpent that has hidden himself among you. You will heal him, and he will be forgiven, for I am Kristophel, the Angel of Sin."

Wings burst into the air behind him. Mighty and golden. Like rays of rising sunshine. A chorus rang out inside her mind, and the sound of her screaming sobs soured the purity of the music.

She fell back, her body once again under her own control. Rose didn't have to tell her this time. She turned and ran.

The door seemed a mile away. A bad dream of slow motion. Her mind sang a single note of alarm into the emptiness of her understanding, and the angel's light grew to searing heat that burned the skin on the back of her neck.

The doorknob was under her hand, but it wouldn't turn. She brought her fist down on it. Slapped her hand flat against the door. Screamed for help, but the feeble noise she made was a whisper compared to the hum of power coming from the creature behind her.

She turned and pressed herself flat. Beat her head against the solid wood as a bitter wind pulled air from her lungs.

Kristophel held the scrap of cloth in front of him. It glowed with the same light as his skin. Deeper and brighter. Piercing shafts shot from his fist that sparked off the walls.

His wings stretched to their limits, and with a roar, he blasted higher into the air. The downward force drove into the mattress, and the bedframe collapsed with a crash.

He shot forward on the force of his flight, and his bulk filled her field of view until all she could see was the light.

His fist struck her in the chest. She felt the ribs and lungs crush into the door. Felt the door splinter. Felt the cool air of the hallway outside wash over her sweating brow.

Blood gurgled through her scream, and she lacked the breath to clear it from her throat. She looked up into the glittering eyes of the Viazo Grand dragon, and listened to the beating of wings.

"No matter what," Rose said, "you'll always have me. Even if you *are* talking to your dead sister, you weirdo. Of course, you're dead too now, so there's that."

She was on something slimy and unsteady. Like the floor was uncured Jell-O. Light bounced around her like sun reflecting off of rippling water.

Was this just her brain coping with death? The last electrical impulses of a dying organ?

The perfect plaster of the ceiling cracked and peeled. Flaked off in chunks to reveal another layer of rot and filth beneath it. The slimy floor rose up to surround her, and it was as black as used motor oil.

It was full of bugs. Swimming insects with sharp legs and jagged skin. They cut and slashed and forced their way inside her as more of the ceiling fell away.

Eyes. There were eyes everywhere, and like the bugs flowing into her blood to meet in the center, the eyes coalesced into two glowing orbs. Not the gaze of the Arktis, but something far more evil. Older than the dragon could ever be. A face hung above. Watching her die with intense curiosity.

The bugs reached her heart, but she was now full of light. Deep in her soul where only Rose had ever been. As the bugs were burned away, fleeing in screaming hordes, the face smiled.

The smiling face became the angel's, but he was suddenly just a man. Not the great hulking presence from before, but a man lifting her head to his chest, rocking her back and forth. Lifting her into his arms.

He murmured into her ear. Some prayer she couldn't understand.

He carried her into the night.

When she reached for Rose, her sister wasn't there. The loneliness that settled in her chest was worse than anything she had ever felt. Instead of waiting to die, she hoped for it, and for the first time since Rose died all those years ago, she was tempted to pray.

But the angel had done enough of it for both of them.

Chapter Three

HER MOUTH TASTED LIKE SAND. The way the beach smelled in the early morning. Wet from dew and the receding tide.

Mickayla stretched. Shuddered through a jaw-popping yawn. When the usual morning cough failed to hit, she opened her eyes in confusion.

Her lungs were clear. No liquid rasping. No raw scratching in the back of the throat. After a couple of years of smoking — from sneaking out behind the shed to filling the ashtray on the front porch in plain sight to two and a half packs a day — she couldn't remember the last time she hadn't coughed herself awake.

The smoker's alarm clock.

She pulled the sheets up to her chin. Smooth under her fingertips. The rough edge of the lace border tickled her palm.

She held herself still. Slid her hands along the fabric until they met over her breastbone. The whorls of her fingerprints seemed to lock into place. Her fingertips were no longer numb. Dead and dumb at the ends of her arms.

She sat up with a gasp. Threw her legs over the side of the bed. *Her* bed. Where was Room Number Three?

She expected Rose to answer her with some snide comment, but her sister remained silent. Maybe she was as confused as Mickayla was.

She looked behind her as she reached for the Smolders on the nightstand. The other side of the bed was rumpled. A depression sunk into the mattress. As if a large *somebody* had been there during the night.

She put her hand on the other pillow. It was soft and cool. Little cotton pulls rolling under her thumb.

Whoever it had been was gone.

Noise from the kitchen made her snatch her hand to her chest and turn toward the door. Soft clicks. A deep breath.

It wasn't Carl. He always sounded like he was growling.

She pulled a cigarette from the pack and stood. Thumbed the Bic open and squinted against the light of the blue flame.

The cigarette tasted like shit. Like the first one she had ever smoked. Her sinuses burned, and she shook her head in disgust.

She didn't bother with clothes. She took another drag through her sneering lips and threw the door open.

It was the maniac from the Viazo Grand. In a flash of staggering memory, she saw him. Only ... less. He looked more like a college linebacker than a titan. He was naked, and his skin glistened with a thin sheen of sweat. His hair tumbled to his hunched shoulders as he bent forward at the kitchen table. Focused on the placemat in front of him.

She took another drag. Less harsh. Not as hot. She nodded as she stepped around the table to lean on the counter. All she remembered was ... confusion. Light and sound. Like a bad trip. Her cancer had spread to her brain. Made her hallucinate.

What started as a good time at the hotel ended up as a good time at her apartment. She shook her head. What the hell was the guy's name again?

Rose still didn't answer.

She finished the cigarette in silence. Watched him with a confused smile.

He was playing with LEGOs. With exact care. Looking at the small booklet of instructions. Placing each plastic block with precision. Tiny bits of color in his big hands.

She stubbed the cigarette out. Lit a fresh one. "Enjoying yourself?"

He nodded, and his hair brushed across the toy sculpture. It looked like a pirate ship. Cannons and masts. He was working on the crow's nest.

"Where'd you get 'em?"

"I stole them."

She turned to grab her valium. Shook a couple into her palm. "Grown man stealing LEGOs?"

She popped the pills into her mouth. Held the cigarette to the side and reached for a glass to fill with water.

"I need to know the sin before I can see it in others."

She paused with her hand sitting on the faucet. That sounded familiar. When Rose didn't offer any insight, she turned the water on, and in the rush of sound, a memory formed.

She worked the pills into her cheek with her tongue. "So you can forgive them, right?"

His face was in shadow, but she could still see his smile. "Bingo," he said.

"Wait a minute." She tried to remember more, but it was like looking through frosted glass. "Weren't you more … formal yesterday? Like a preacher or something?"

He leaned back. Held the ship up. Grinned at her with teeth so white it looked like his mouth was lit from within.

She nodded and rolled her eyes. "Good job, buddy." She brought the glass of water to her lips.

"I would not do that," he said.

She swallowed the pills in one gulp. Smacked her lips and stuck her tongue out to show him her mouth was empty. "Wouldn't do what?" she said.

Where the fuck was Rose?

He set the pirate ship aside and shrugged. "You should not commit sin against yourself."

She took a deep drag of the cigarette. Blew the smoke out of her nose. "Why not?"

"Because I healed you."

"Really? Why does every guy think his dick is the cure for cancer?"

She leaned back in confusion. That was a weird thing to say. Something Rose would have said to *her*. Not something she would ever have said out loud.

"I misspoke," he said. "Because the *Remnant of Bethsaida* has healed you. It has made you pure."

A cramp formed at the base of her throat. The burn of bubbling acid. She held her hand up like trying to pause the conversation. "I don't really remember much of what happened yesterday after the doctor told me I was gonna die." She winced and turned away when the cramp twisted in her gut. The burning travelled up her throat like vomit.

"The power is inside you now," he said.

She held up the finger again. Followed it with a snarling glare. He only sat and watched.

"Why don't you—" she gasped. Caught her breath and swallowed. "Put some fucking clothes on."

She barely got the words out before her throat opened, and her mouth was flooded with bile.

She dropped her cigarette on the tile and bent forward with both hands pushed into her abdomen. Her howling voice gurgled through the stream. A glittering flood of thick black liquid.

Like the oil she had been suspended in while something great and awful floated above her in judgement. She pulled in a burning breath, and braced for a fresh gout. Where it hit the floor, it bubbled and hissed. Sank through the grout. Ran in rivulets to disappear in the sandy texture.

Another breath, and she dropped to her knees, but the only thing to come out the third time was her ragged scream.

Her heart pounded, and she couldn't catch her breath. She felt the biting itch of insects trying to get inside her, and she jumped up with a cry of revulsion.

There was nothing there.

She covered her face and cried into her hands. "The fuck?" she said. "The fuck is wrong with me?"

"Child. Look at me."

The chair creaked as he stood. She shook her head, but her fingers separated, and she opened her eyes.

He stood as he had at the hotel. Revealed in the glory of another form. Glowing wings and beauty, but … like when she first saw him sitting at her kitchen table … he was diminished.

She fell back against the counter as the memories rushed back into her head, and even when she closed her eyes, she could still see his light. But it wasn't as bright. As gold. Cooling even as her knees buckled, and she threw her hands out to grab the counter to keep from falling over.

She opened her eyes, and he stood there as a man. She reached out for him. "Kristophel?"

He smiled. Nodded as he stepped forward to take her hand. "Yes, child."

"What is happening to me?"

He pulled her into his arms. Pressed her cheek into his chest. "You have been imbued with the power of the Christ. That divine spark which transferred health through contact. Not the active spark. Not the one He used with will and intent, but the *passive* spark. That which just ... was."

"Was what?" she whispered.

"It was His essence. Too powerful to be contained inside a human form."

She pushed away from him. Looked down to keep from stepping in the black goo, but there was nothing there. Did she imagine that too?

No. It was as real as the crashing memories of the light spreading throughout her body. The pain of healing. The terror of judgement.

The pack of Smolders crinkled in her hands, and she looked back over her shoulder. "Will I puke this shit out again?"

He shook his head. "Though still a sin, they damage over time. There will be a price, but not immediate."

"What, like I'll be walking down the street and just lean to the side and york up that black stuff into the gutter?"

He pointed a finger gun at her. "Bingo."

She got a cigarette in her mouth, but she couldn't keep the flame steady enough to light it. Kristophel glided forward and took the lighter from her hands. Lit her cigarette. Fished one out for himself, and they stood that way for several minutes. Sinning. Breathing in each other's smoke.

She pointed at the lighter. "Don't steal that."

He shook his head. "Never. I have already sinned enough against friends."

"Right, so what's going on?"

It would be nice if Rose would speak up. Any time now ...

"I told you."

"You said I was healed. That you looked for thousands of years for me. Something about following threads."

He looked down with an embarrassed smile. "I was very high at the time. I think I was trying to extend a metaphor."

"A metaphor for what?"

"For how lives are woven into time. Like a cloth is woven with individual threads."

"Like the Remnant of Beth's Uncle?"

"*Bethsaida*."

"The hell is that?"

He pulled the dwindling pack of cigarettes into his hand and walked back to his chair at the table. His muscles rippled under his skin, unobscured by body fat. She tried to remember if anything happened in her bed last night.

Nothing but sleepless dreams.

Rose would probably think that was too bad ... if she ever bothered waking up.

"Christ and His disciples often walked through villages. Many of these villages were full of non-believers. Diseased sinners. Christ wanted to heal these people. He desperately wanted to make every man, woman, and child whole and healthy."

"So why didn't he?"

Kristophel shrugged. "It was His form. He could only hold as much of the divine spark as His form on earth could tolerate."

"So, he had to pick and choose?"

Kristophel shook his head. "No. He let the spark flow out of him regardless of the taker."

"So the remnant is ..."

"It is a scrap from the hem of his cloak he wore in the village of Bethsaida. His divine spark was running out, as was his time on earth, but the people kept taking. Taking what He no longer gave." Kristophel held his hands up as if she were about to object. "He was not withholding healing from anyone who *asked*, but they stopped asking. Just taking. Without listening to His word. Without bringing the power of His gospel into their hearts and minds. They no longer waited for Him to touch them, but instead rushed to take what was not offered."

She no longer wanted to be standing there naked, but she wanted to hear the rest. She frowned in sympathy. "That sounds awful."

"It was. For He so loved mankind, it tore at His being to deny them. But there was the final ascension. There was still a great sermon to deliver, so He shed the robes, and walked naked into the desert to pray. In His absence, the disciples were met by a mob. Villagers desperate for healing. If just by His touch they could be healed, what of a brush with his robes. A blind man was given sight just by reaching out to run his fingers through the frayed ends of his cloak. After the villagers were through, the only thing that remained of his clothes was a scrap of fabric, and even that had enough of the divine spark to heal many many men ... or one who was beyond such power."

She folded her arms over her breasts. "So where is it now?"

He pointed at her. "It is in you."

She dropped her arms back to her side. "I'm sorry?"

"The power is in *you*. You have been cured of your cancer. Purified in God's eyes. You carry Christ's divine spark."

She held up one of her hands. "Wait a minute. you

said it was greater than … the *form* he took. Greater than a human body."

"Correct."

"Then how can I …" She trailed off. Clipped the question behind clenched teeth. "Where is Rose?"

He looked down at his hands. His skin wasn't dark enough to cover his shame. "She is why you can hold the spark."

"What are you saying? Where is she?"

"Her soul was intermingled with yours."

The price of this cure was to lose her sister again? "No fucking way. Bring her back!"

"Only you can do that."

"How?"

"By getting her back from the one that took her."

She remembered the floating eyes above her at the Viazo Grand. The bugs tearing at her flesh. The wicked smile as she faded away. "Who took her?"

"The one you must heal."

"Give me an answer, God damn it!"

"Blasphemy is a sin."

"Fuck you!"

She lunged from the counter. Drove her hands into his shoulder. "Who took my sister? Who do I have to heal, you son of a bitch?"

He looked down at the floor. Clasped his hands in front of him as if he was going to pray. "To get your sister free of eternal damnation, you must heal the devil himself. The Father of Sin is dying."

Chapter Four

KRISTOPHEL TRIED to follow her into the bedroom. Hands up and explaining. She slammed the door in his face.

His voice droned on as she got dressed. Put her hair in a ponytail. Grabbed her purse and jerked the door open on his big surprised face.

She squeezed past him, picked up the cigarettes and lighter, and was at the foyer before he could complete his last sentence.

Something about two being one, and the divine plan.

"Put some fucking pants on," she said before slamming the door.

She stood in the hallway with her head back. Deep breaths that smelled like carpet shampoo. He hadn't tried to follow her. Maybe he was getting dressed. Getting ready to come after her.

She pushed off and turned left at the elevators. No way was she going to get caught inside with one of her neighbors. Frank Gerber from 7C. Mrs. Halsey in the corner apartment. Clutching her ratty purse to the front of her caftan. "I told them not to trim the hedges so early. It scares the birds."

Her sneakers squealed on the steps as she skipped down. The polished wooden railing felt like glass. A door slammed above her, and she quickened her pace.

She hit the bottom and paused to catch her breath — only she didn't need to. Instead of pounding through her ribs like usual, her heart was calm and steady.

Maybe she *was* healed.

She snorted laughter and stepped into the lobby. Past an empty desk that hinted at days gone by where a doorman may have waited. Now it was full of pamphlets and flyers.

She lit a cigarette before the glass door wheezed shut behind her. Squinted through the billow of smoke. The small lot across the street was surrounded by rusting chain link. Her spot was empty.

"Fuck!" she shouted.

A lady in a black felt coat looked away as she passed. Pulled her collar up to her ears. Quickened her pace and threw a concerned look over her shoulder.

This was where Rose would have piped up with a joke. Some piece of sarcastic wisdom. Mickayla shook her head. Turned to face in the opposite direction of the judgmental pedestrian.

Took off with her head down. Reached for the pack of cigarettes before realizing she already had one going.

"This is bullshit, Rose."

A long drag. Turned right at the corner.

"You should be here. Unless there *is* no here."

She looked up at a group of people waiting for the light to change at the next corner. She curled her lip in a silent growl. Cut into an alley next to the laundry. Tracked along the back of her building.

Another right at the end, and she threw the crumbling butt into the gutter. Went through the next traffic light instead of turning right again. No sense in doing laps.

North. Always north.

Toward the hotel where her car might still be? Toward the lake where her sister might be?

"Maybe there *is* no car. Or *lake*."

"Excuse me?"

She looked up into the polite gaze of a man standing next to a taxi. Driver or passenger, she couldn't tell. Slick hair. Leather gloves. Sport coat.

She pointed her cigarette at him. "You know, I'm probably dying."

He took a half step back, and his face went from *can I help you* to *can somebody help me* in a single breath.

Mickayla shook her head. "Not in an imminent way, but like right now. All this is just the last gasp of my consciousness. The final synapse protecting my fragile psyche from the pain of …" She flapped her hand at him, and he flinched away. "The tunnel of light or whatever," she finished.

His eyes widened as he shook his head. He eased around the front bumper and opened the door. "Why are the pretty ones always fucked up?"

He dropped in, and the engine turned over. So, he was either the driver or he was stealing it. She looked away as he pulled into traffic. Caught the eye of a guy in a velour tracksuit. "That's a good question," she said.

He didn't answer, so she shrugged. Lit another cigarette. Dropped her head and crossed the street without looking at the lights.

Orange and brown leaves skittered into her path. Let her know she was well away from the businesses and schools. The docks and clubs.

Concrete gave way to grass. Bushes and trees loomed like wooden skeletons. The sun peeked through the clouds directly overhead, and the grays turned to vibrant color.

She hooked her finger into the pack of Smolders only to find it empty. She crumpled it and dropped it on the ground next to the border of a parking lot that looked like hardening lava.

A blight amidst nature's attempt to push the city away.

She reached into her purse for the other pack she hoped would be there, and her diaphragm hitched. Her gasp sounded like a kid blowing bubbles into his school lunch milk carton.

Her abs tightened, and the cough erupted from her lungs like air from a burst balloon. Her vision clouded over, and she dropped to her knees.

She couldn't breath. Couldn't get a deep enough breath to satisfy her need for oxygen. Or deep enough to expel the sin from her lungs.

And that's what it was. Sin. Willfully harming herself. Treating her body like an ashtray instead of a temple.

She pulled in a whooping breath that was cool and sweet, and the cloud over her eyes became light. A solid sheet that burst apart into swimming pinpoints, and she saw the wriggling black goo of the evil she had done to herself seep into the grass.

A trail of drool hung from her lips. She pulled it away with shaking fingers and sat back on her heels. Took deep breaths. Settled into a new rhythm.

There was a bench a few yards away. Covered in fallen leaves. A metal trash can with an ashtray on top. Perfect.

She stood with a grunt. Wiped the tears away with the back of her hand. Rose's silence was like a chill wind at her back. Like a blanket falling off in the night. Waking up cold. She pulled her collar closed and sat down with a sigh.

How could she miss a person that had only existed in her head? Well, after she died, anyway.

She took her time opening the new pack of Smolders. Slid the first one free, and when she lit it, just like this morning, it tasted like the first one she'd ever had.

Jenny Stalz had given her one of her mother's cigarettes. New Eve Lite 100's. "You're not even inhaling it," she had squealed in her honking cartoon voice. Swollen adenoids and braces.

Mickayla had taken a big drag. Breathed in the smoke while looking Jenny in the eye. The pounding heart and swimmy head were amazing, and she was hooked from the first one.

She finally looked up and leaned back, blowing smoke into the air above her head. She was next to the overflow parking lot of the Burg Spires Church of Hope.

The shock of seeing the church made her slump over her purse in disbelief. How many miles was the church from her building?

Ten miles? Twelve?

Rose would have said something exactly like that. After all, she was a figment of her imagination, right?

The church was both old and new. The age of each additional structure tracking its existence through time.

The old brick from before the railroads. Crumbling plaster. The new brick from after Prohibition, when the boats started running more than whiskey. Stone and iron from the middle of America.

The wall of stained glass. The humble rectory.

Burg Spires was a forgotten landmark. Important to the history of a city that built its foundations on an oppressed people, but too close to the sins of founding fathers to stay in the limelight.

The once great church had faded from view, and the

cracks in the asphalt of the parking lot made her wonder how long it would be before the earth took back what belonged to it.

Soft steps in the grass to the left. Her heart jumped into panic mode, and she drew her feet in. A woman alone, even next to a church?

Rose would tell her how stupid she had been. How she was a buffet for the deviants of the world.

The steps belonged to a young man. Dark hair hanging in sweaty strands. Shirt dampened with his effort. Jogging with a sure stride.

Something about the way he smiled to himself put her at ease. She relaxed as he approached.

He looked up from his path, and his smile opened into a grin when he saw her. He slowed to stand next to the bench, and his grin faded into concern. "Hello," he said. His voice was soft and gentle. Deep and soothing. "I don't mean to intrude, but a pretty lady crying outside my church tends to grab my attention."

She pressed the heels of both hands into her eyes. They came away soaked. She sniffed, and looked back up at the young man in surprise. "I didn't know I was crying."

He spread his hands. "All the more reason for me to ask." He pointed at the empty space beside her. "May I?"

She nodded. Dug into her purse for a tissue while he sat. Too many things in her hands. Purse, lighter, tissue, cigarette. She worked it all out. Like a jumbled puzzle falling into place, and she wadded the used tissue into her pocket. "I'm sorry," she said in a harsh whisper.

He flapped his hand in dismissal. "No, no. It's quite alright."

She chuckled with a rueful shake of her head. Pointed at the church with her cigarette. "*Your* church? I thought the guy who ran this one was an old fat guy. Borders or Banker or something."

The young man's concern became the smile again. "*Binder*. Pastor Binder *was* tasked with this mission, but he was called home."

Mickayla took a drag. Blew the smoke out the side of her mouth. "What, did he have a sick mother or something?"

The young man laughed. "I'm so sorry, but no. The *Lord* called him home."

She shook her head in confusion, and then gasped in embarrassment. "Oh … oh, he *died*. I'm so stupid."

"Of course not. You are in distress. It's easy to make that kind of mistake. Again, I sincerely apologize for laughing. Here. Let's begin again."

He extended his hand. "My name is Owen. I'm the new pastor here at the Burg Spires Church of Hope."

She hesitated. Instead of taking his hand, she waved. Like her hand was a fluttering moth. "Mickayla Waters. Burg City prostitute."

He didn't snatch his hand away. Just settled it back in his lap with a small nod and that accepting smile. It was almost enough to make her start crying again.

"Pardon me for saying, but you seem very young for such a profession," he said.

"I could say the same about you."

He inclined his head. "Yes, but I'm not crying outside of a church."

She took another drag and blew the smoke through her nose. "My day is not going exactly as I planned."

"Maybe not *your* plan, perhaps."

She remembered Kristophel and his divine plan nonsense. *Whose* plan were they talking about? "Father … sir … what do I call you?"

"You can call me Owen."

She stubbed out the cigarette and slid a fresh one from the pack. He didn't say anything. Only watched her light up. Waited until she was ready. She chuckled. "You should have seen me a few minutes ago. I puked my sin all over your grass. Like squirming oil."

His eyebrow twitched, and he leaned slightly forward. Suddenly more engaged in what she was saying. He nodded. "Smoking *does* cause problems."

She smiled around the cigarette. Pulled in a fresh drag. "Kristophel told me it's a sin. Now *that's* a problem."

His polite smile froze. There was a wet click when he swallowed. "Kristophel?"

"Yeah, he said he was the Angel of Sin."

His sweat no longer looked healthy. His skin was pale and gray, and the moisture made him look sick. Like he was suffering from a bad fever. "Did he say anything else?"

She looked away from his eyes. They no longer seemed inviting. "He said I was healed. Said I had it in me now. Not sure *what*, but it's in me." She wanted to tell him about Rose. Opened her mouth to start, only he interrupted her with a breathless whisper.

"The spark."

She nodded and pointed at him. "That's right. That's what he said."

"And you are to use it?"

She collapsed in relief. Tension she wasn't even aware of flowed away. "Yes. From the Remnant of Bethesda or something."

"Bethsaida?"

Her excitement grew. Either she wasn't crazy after all, or her hallucination was much more clever than she imagined. "Yes! And he said I was supposed to heal—"

He slapped his hand on the planks next to his leg. "Say

no more. Do not blaspheme here. Do *not* ..." He trailed away with a trembling finger aimed at her chest.

She sat back in shock. The savage anger on his face looked like a strained mask.

He launched to his feet. Smoothed his damp t-shirt. Took a deep breath. "If you would like, I can recommend the names of several professionals who can help with your mental issues. I am not qualified or prepared for such counseling."

She looked up at him with her mouth hanging open. Fresh tears blurred his image into a mass of shifting color.

He turned away. "Then I suggest you find help on your own. I'm sorry, but you won't find it here."

He turned and walked to the edge of the parking lot. Before stepping off the grass, he slowed. Looked back at her over his shoulder. "Never come back to this church."

His feet on the asphalt sounded like waves lapping against the rotting wood of the family dock. Receding into the distance as she sank below the surface.

She had no idea what Rose would have said to that.

Chapter Five

THE BURG-HEARTSTONE BRIDGE. With its filthy birds and the stench of garbage blowing up from the endless line of trash barges.

Zoos and rich people and high-end coffee shops on one side. Liquor stores and poor people and fast-food restaurants on the other.

From Sloppy's to filet mignon in one trip. Including the toll.

The traffic behind her made the bridge thrum like it had a heartbeat. She stood at the rusty railing. Looked out at the setting sun turning the muddy water into reflected fire.

She'd brought the Zippo's flame up to the cigarette at least ten times, but never touched the tip.

In school, she would direct Rose's attention to one student or another. Silent derision, and Rose would say, "I wonder if their mother ever had any kids that lived?"

Was it her sister's question or her own? Was Rose only there as a figment of her imagination?

She looked down at the water so far below her feet.

Wondered if it was far enough to kill her if she jumped. Pointed her head straight down and put her hands behind her back.

The whoosh of air, and then WHAM!

Glittering bubbles. Seaweed swaying in the current. She would settle deeper into the dark, and a small hand would fill hers.

She sighed around the cigarette. Brought the flame up one more time, but her silent sobs made it impossible to hit the mark. She crossed her arms and hunched her shoulders. The cigarette fell from her snotty lips. Something she wouldn't have felt yesterday. Maybe not even a month ago.

If the angel playing with LEGOs in her apartment was to be believed, she was healed. Cured of the cancer that was going to kill her as completely as the rushing water of Lake Winstead had killed her sister.

How could that be true?

Long conversations with Rose deep into the night where they asked each other if God was real. And if he was, how could he possibly be a kind and benevolent God if he let such shitty things happen to his children.

Why let a crack baby die knowing nothing but the pain of withdrawal?

Why let an innocent person get shot in a drive-by?

Why did war exist?

Why did cancer?

Why take one twin, and not the other? Instead of or at the same time ... But then the parents would suffer.

And the children would never know a life of the joy that could be had. Or the misery to be suffered.

Or the loneliness.

She slid to her knees. Pressed her face into the gap between the steel rods of the bridge's railing. The steps of passersby hurried to carry them away from her. Sympathetic sighs. Disapproving whispers.

Not a single hand on her shoulder to see if she was okay.

This fucking city …

Without the comfort of her sister's voice in her ear, it seemed even colder. Darker. Nothing to be had in this stinking city but the promise of another shitty day.

Pastor Owen had looked at her like she was a leper. Her mouth twitched in a smile. That was a joke Rose would have liked.

"Fuck this," she said.

She pulled the cigarettes out of her purse. If she had Christ's healing power inside her, there was no point in them anymore.

They didn't give her the same buzz, they tasted like asshole, and truth be told, she only smoked them to punish herself.

The whole reason she got out of bed in the first place.

She held them out and opened her hand. The pack fell, spinning and tumbling. Cigarettes flew out to create a broken spiral, and it all fluttered out of sight.

Too far away to hear if they made a splash. Imagining them splatting on the surface made her jealous. They would soak, break apart, and scatter into the depths.

She clinked the Zippo closed and dropped it back in her purse. Heaved herself to her feet and squared her shoulders. When she took a deep breath, she wondered if her body would heal from all the cigarettes she had smoked since crawling away from Burg Spires or if she'd bring up another load of maggoty oil.

She slung her purse and was surprised at her own smile. What the fuck was there to be happy about? She shrugged and turned back toward town.

Now she was talking to herself … but hadn't she always?

She threw her head back and laughed. The other people walking with her veered away like they were magnets and she was their opposite pole.

She was done walking by the time she got to Jefferson Avenue. She had stopped crying blocks ago, so she hailed a cab. Fifty bucks seemed a decent alternative to the subway and another couple miles under the bare tree limbs hanging over the road on the way to the hotel.

The cabbie was a small white guy named Franklin who looked like he was trying to eat his own face. "Mind if I listen to the radio? They gotta Hall & Oates marathon going on Burg FM. I think they're about up to the M's and I really like *Maneater*."

She waved her permission and looked out the window as the cab filled with blue-eyed soul.

When they got to the Viazo Grand, she asked him to take her around back, and he winked in the rearview mirror. Maybe it wasn't the first time he dropped a girl like her off where the workers hid from the guests.

She tipped him a twenty and closed the door on a rambling *thank you* that included, "You should stay for the next one. *North Star's* pretty good."

Her car was still there, but Amanda's Lincoln was gone. It seemed calmer than usual back there. No bustle of deliveries. No click-clack of heels from another girl going for a smoke.

She dropped into the driver's seat, and like always, the Subaru started right up. Best purchase she had ever made, even if it looked like it was ready for the compactor. As she pulled out, she reached down for a cigarette.

They were with Rose now.

She rolled the window down anyway. Turned the radio

on. Found Burg FM and listened all the way to *Out of Touch* before pulling into her spot across from her building.

She didn't take the elevator this time. She wasn't tired. In fact, she felt better than she had in … years maybe. She was just bored with being on her feet. Bored with crying and feeling sorry for herself.

The building seemed empty. Nobody in the elevator. Nobody in the hallway when she stepped out. No loud TVs. Shouted conversations.

Her door opened without the key, and when she entered, Kristophel looked up from the kitchen table. He saw it was her. Inclined his head in a slow nod of greeting before going back to inspecting whatever was holding his attention.

She looked at the refrigerator, but she wasn't hungry. Nothing felt like it would be very satisfying, until her gaze fell on the wine rack.

She walked over to the table. "Hey."

Kristophel looked back up. Blinked his eyes as if coming awake. A pill bottle sat near his hand. Open and on its side. She pointed at it. "Is that my valium?"

His grin was lopsided. "They were, yes."

"You took *all* of them?"

He gave her the same awkward finger gun from the morning. "Bingo."

"Sinning it up, huh?"

"I must commit it to know it … so I can find it … yes."

She sighed. "I got a question."

He leaned back and spread his hands. "I am listening."

"If I drink some wine, will it come out of me like the apocalypse?"

His eyebrows drew down. "I don't understand."

"Remember when I coughed up some Texas best?"

He closed his eyes. "Yes. The cleansing."

"Right. So, will that happen if I get a little buzz?"

He shrugged. "How would one know?"

She looked up at the ceiling. "I guess we'll both find out soon enough."

When she popped the cork a few minutes later, the buttery aroma of the pinot hit her nose in a wave strong enough to make her forget about everything she had ever smelled.

She rolled her eyes in pleasure before even taking a sip. "You know," she said, "I went to a church."

"Really," he said. He looked more aware than he had just moments ago. Maybe he was going through his own cleansing.

"Yeah, but it was by accident."

"Rarely are there accidents."

"Whatever. I talked to a pastor about you."

He sat like stone for several moments. Finally, he looked up. Like the way a child tries to be casual. "And what did he say?"

"He turned me away. Told me to get professional help."

Kristophel drew back in confusion. "That is a curious reaction."

"I thought so." She looked down and realized her glass was already empty. As she poured another serving she watched his eyes. They gave nothing away except for a subtle worry.

"Did you touch him?" he asked.

"Nope."

"Perhaps that was why."

"Why what?"

He pointed to the wine. "May I have a glass of that?"

She shrugged. "Sure, but you're gonna have to pour it yourself. I'm not your wife."

SAWYER BLACK & DAVID W. WRIGHT

He leaned forward, and the chair groaned under his weight. He squinted up at her. Nodded to himself as if he saw something in her that he had been wondering about.

Where he stood and walked around the table, she saw he was still naked. She drained her second glass. Whistled at him like the construction workers hanging out of the arcade windows on 47th. "You really were created in God's image."

He chose a bottle. Another red. "As were we all."

She watched him open and pour, and when he turned to face her, she said, "You wanna go to bed?"

He shook his head. "I am sorry, but no. That's a sin I've already experienced."

"Suit yourself," she said. She turned and walked to the bedroom as if she hadn't a care in the world. She closed the door and leaned her head against the cool wood.

If she didn't care, why did his rejection hurt so much?

Chapter Six

KRISTOPHEL FILLED her little car with too much person. Hunched over drawn-up knees. Even with his arms crossed, she had to lean to the left to keep from brushing against him.

After last night, she didn't want to touch him. Even accidentally.

She pointed to where the seatbelt should have crossed his thick chest. "I guess breaking the law is technically a sin, right? Even one as dumb as wearing a seatbelt."

"That is correct."

"You know, if we get stopped, *I'm* the one that gets the ticket."

He didn't even look at her.

She shrugged. "Fine. We'll just tell him you got a note from your doctor. Claustrophobia or something."

"Lying is a sin."

"No shit."

The suspension creaked when they pulled into the Viazo Grand parking lot. "You know all about the sin of lying, though, don't you?"

"I do."

She rolled her eyes as she drove around to the rear. Amanda's Lincoln was back in its accustomed spot, and she slid the Subaru in next to it. Close enough to give Kristophel trouble getting out.

She grabbed her purse and left him to struggle, but when she got to the hedges hiding the back door, she glanced up to find him at her side. She hid her surprise by searching for the brass key. "You teleport or something?"

"I am just *here*." He sounded bored.

She opened the secret door to the sound of construction. Hammers and saws. Muted shouts and music.

The upper railing next to Amanda's office was blocked by hanging plastic. Plaster dust filled the air. A drop cloth was taped down over the crimson carpet all the way up the stairs.

She looked up like she was talking to Arktis. "What happened?"

Kristophel stepped around her to answer for the dragon. "I was not myself."

She remembered the dark smile hanging above her. The splintered burning in her chest. She looked up at Kristophel's sheepish smile. "This was you?"

He shook his head. "It was the transfer of the divine spark. When the Remnant of Bethsaida was discharged, there was some … damage."

Her time in Room Number Three was hazy. Snippets and snatches. Even the last words she remembered Rose saying were just noise. She wondered if Rose had *ever* talked to her.

Was her whole memory broken? Was all this *really* a projection of her dying brain?

That would be where Rose told her to stop fucking

around. Or maybe not. She wasn't sure of *anything* anymore.

Kristophel seemed content to look at the progress of the remodeling, so she steered around him and headed to the stairs. The tarp was slick with dust, and she had to grab the rail with both hands.

The office door was open, and when Mickayla stepped through the doorway, Amanda looked up from her desk. Her mouth opened, but before she spoke, her eyes widened, and she leaned back. Her gaze tracked past Mickayla's shoulder.

She turned to see what had spooked her, and Kristophel rose up the stairs as if he was levitating. She remembered him hovering over the bed. Her heart trying to tear itself from her chest.

She turned back to Amanda with a shrug. "Can we come in?"

Amanda blinked. "Fucking hell. What am I to do? Of course you can fucking come in."

Mickayla crossed to a chair on the other side of Amanda's desk. The air seemed to compress when Kristophel came in. The lamp dimmed at the memory of the light under his skin.

Amanda rose. Smoothed the back of her skirt. Brushed hair back from her forehead. Mickayla stared. She couldn't believe that her friend was nervous.

Amanda pointed to the other seat next to Mickayla. "Please. This is not my house, but I welcome you into *this* wing that is under my dominion."

Kristophel bowed. "You welcomed me previously, but I am minister of fire and flame. By His grace, I accept."

He sat with formality, and only when he was situated did Amanda sit as well.

Mickayla looked from one to the other. "What is going

on here?"

Amanda laid her hands flat on her desk. "He's a fucking angel, darling. An *angel*. In the *Viazo Grand*."

"I get it … wait a minute. How do you know that?"

"Are you fucking simple? I tried to tell you as much when I called you in here two days ago. I tried—"

"Bullshit. You just trembled and smoked."

"Speaking of which, do you have a fag, darling?"

"What? No. I quit."

Kristophel snickered.

Mickayla turned to face him. "What's so funny? Thanks to you, I can't smoke without choking on … whatever that shit is."

He steepled his fingers in front of his chest. "It is the physical manifestation of spiritual corruption."

"Yeah, well, it looks like the greasy shits."

Amanda held up her hand. "Just a moment." She aimed her attention at Kristophel. "You were rather cryptic, if you forgive one for saying so."

Kristophel nodded in acquiescence.

Amanda continued. "But you made it clear that you were going to be her last … client."

"And I was."

Mickayla spread her hands. "How do you figure?"

"Darling, please," Amanda said. "I thought you had stormed out and left the hotel. Imagine my chagrin when a being of pure golden light smashed through the wall with your bloody corpse in his arms."

"It wasn't her corpse," Kristophel said.

Mickayla scooted to the front of the chair. "Excuse me?"

Amanda held her hand up for silence. "Then whose was it?"

Kristophel lifted his right fist. "When I penetrated

her—"

"Gross," Mickayla shouted.

He glanced at her in disgust. "With the *Remnant of Bethsaida*—"

He was interrupted again, but this time by Amanda jumping from her seat. She pushed away from the desk, and her chair flew back to hit the wall behind her. "My God," she whispered.

Mickayla shrugged. "That seems to be the prevailing sentiment."

Amanda's hands rose to her mouth. She held them over her lips like she was trying to keep her voice inside. She stared at Kristophel with horror.

Her distress made Mickayla catch her breath. She stood and walked around the desk. Held her hands up to pull the other woman into her arms.

Amanda shrieked and flung herself away. Stumbled back and flapped her hands like she was shooing away a cloud of flues. "Don't touch me!" she gasped.

Mickayla froze. "What? Amanda, what is it?"

"Don't you understand?" Amanda's eyes were white all around her pale iris. Her skin was pallid, and the veins stood out in her neck. "The touch of the Christ — the divine spark of life doesn't just *cure* you. It *purifies* you."

Mickayla shook her head and stepped forward.

Amanda jammed herself into the corner. "Don't!"

Mickayla relented. Stepped back in confusion.

Amanda straightened. Clasped her hands in front of her navel. "It *absolves* you. Don't you understand? It *forgives* you of all your sins. Until you sin again, you can be *seen*."

She stared at Mickayla in silence. A deep quiet punctuated by the sounds of work in the hallway.

Mickayla turned to Kristophel, but he offered nothing but a raised eyebrow. She threw her hands out with a growl. "This is bullshit. Like I'm supposed to know what that means. What *any* of this means."

She spun on her heels and retraced her steps. Dropped back down into the chair and crossed her arms with an audible *humph*.

Rose would usually tell her to stop acting like a baby. It felt like that may have happened … years ago.

"Darling," Amanda said.

Mickayla kept her eyes on the floor. "What?"

Amanda sighed. Her soft steps brought her back to her place behind the desk. "You are very young. You know so little about this life. How can anyone expect you to know anything about the *after*life?"

"That sounds patronizing."

"That's because it is. You're a fucking child."

"One that fucks for money."

"Be thankful you *aren't* that kind of child."

Mickayla looked up through her hanging bangs. "I've gone through kind of a lot in a couple of days."

Amanda startled her with a belly laugh. "You've seen one angel, and you think you've been through a *lot*? You've been filled with the divine spark. The healing power of the son of God. Do you really think you've seen everything?"

She leaned forward, and her eyes flickered. Like the sheen of a cat's eyes. She brought her hands together. Rotated a silver ring on her first finger. "You have no fucking idea."

Kristophel cleared his throat.

Amanda snapped upright like she had been prodded with a sharp stick. Mickayla looked over.

The angel leaned forward to look up at Amanda. "Do you have one in need?"

Amanda crossed her arms. "There are *many* in need in this place."

"We will only allow for one."

Amanda narrowed her eyes. "You are trying to tie off this thread, aren't you?"

Mickayla held up her hand. "Who? What thread?"

"Yes," Kristophel said.

"And she's the one?"

"I'm right here," Mickayla shouted.

Kristophel nodded. "She is."

Amanda's eyes no longer flickered. They looked like they had filmed over with pure silver. "Are you sure?"

Kristophel leaned back and put his hands flat on his thighs. "Are you such a one to question one such as I?"

Amanda looked down. Mickayla thought she was going to curtsey. "Of course not," Amanda whispered. "Forgive me."

Without looking back up, she rushed out. Mickayla watched her disappear down the stairs. Directed her gaze to Kristophel. "I should be freaking out right now."

He dipped his head. "The remnant cures more than the body. It cures the soul. And it cures the mind."

"What, like I'm crazy?"

"You were."

"You a shrink now?"

He turned to look into her eyes, and she couldn't hold his gaze. "Tell me," he said. "Is it sane to speak to one's dead sister?"

She looked at her fingers. Watched them as they washed and scrubbed. Intertwined and released. She rubbed her sweaty palms on her jeans. "No," she whispered.

"I thought very much the same."

She sat back and crossed her arms again. Still no Rose telling her to grow up. "I liked you better when you were high."

"I've been told so before."

Even with the tarp softening the sound of her high heels, Mickayla heard Amanda coming up the steps. Another sound soon followed. Near marching footsteps.

She stepped through the door with a young man in tow. Jeans and t-shirt. His hat folded in his wringing hands. He was hunched forward and looking at the floor.

"This is the one," Amanda said.

She turned to the young man. Twirled her finger in the air. "Present yourself, Maynard."

He ducked his head. Turned to face Mickayla and Kristophel, and Mickayla clamped her mouth shut against the scream that rose into her throat.

The young man's lower jaw was missing. His upper lip peeled back in a scar that revealed broken teeth. Puckered skin. Inflamed and swollen. It surrounded a hole at the top of his neck. Roping tendrils of thick skin pulled the rest of his face down to show the bright red half-circles behind his lower eyelids.

Amanda indicated the young man with a sweep of her arm. "This is Maynard. He was on an assignment for our Mr. Peterson. Harvesting fairy dust."

Maynard looked down at the floor. Amanda went back behind her desk. Righted her chair. Sat down with regained elegance. "Fairies don't like having their magic stolen. He was captured and hung head first over a Hellhound's cage. It hadn't eaten in quite a while."

Mickayla looked from Amanda to Maynard. Then to Kristophel. "I'm dead. I know it. None of this is real. Fairy dust, are you kidding me?" She pointed at the ruin of the young man's face. "Who needs to fly that bad?"

Amanda shook her head. "That's not what fairy dust is for."

"Sure it is," Mickayla said. "I saw *Peter Pan.*"

"Darling, I think you're missing the point."

"What, that I got my fables all mixed up?"

"Maynard," Kristophel said. "Put your hand out, please."

The young man compiled without question. Looked up with pleading eyes.

Kristophel turned to her. "Take his hand."

She didn't bother asking why. She stood up and grabbed his extended fingers. There was a moment of suspense between the passing of seconds.

Balance and potential.

There was no flash of light. No trumpets. There was only a thing that was, and a thing that *now* was.

She felt something leave her. Like a relieved sigh. She dropped her hand with a shrug, and flinched away when Maynard cried out.

His joy echoed from the ceiling and walls. He whooped. Threw his hat into the air. He was whole and healthy. Healed by the spark that Kristophel had forced into her. Pulled out of her from her touch.

Tears streamed from Maynard's eyes. His perfect teeth gleamed.

Amanda opened the center drawer of her desk. Reached in and sat back. A small gold container sat in her palm. She opened it, and Mickayla thought she was going to powder her nose. Instead, she pulled out two small wads of cloth.

She stuffed one into each ear. Shrugged when she saw Mickayla staring. "Bits of rope that held the horn around Gabriel's neck. They block their song."

Amanda looked over at Kristophel. "Whose song?"

Maynard clasped his hands together. "How can I thank you, ma'am?"

It took a moment before she realized he was talking to

her. Rose would say neither of them were *ma'ams.*

She lifted her hand to wave his thanks away, but paused when she heard the music. A lilting song of some kind. Like it came from everywhere. From the center of her head. The edges of the universe. There were words in the song. She tried to make them out.

She turned to ask Amanda what it was, but Amanda had turned her chair around. Kristophel looked as bored and unconcerned as usual. She looked at Maynard, and he had ceased his dance of gratitude. He stood staring out the office door.

His mouth fell open. His eyes widened in rapture. Light from the hallway lit his face like he looked up at the sun.

I AM COME

The voice rose out of the song. Birthed from creation itself.

FEAR NOT FOR YOU WILL SUFFER NO LONGER

An angel was outside the door. Floating up the stairs. Her robes and wings fluttering in an unseen wind. Gleaming armor over flowing silk.

A magnificent sword in one hand, a silver net in the other.

FALL INTO ME AND BE REBORN

She spread her net, and Maynard lifted his arms, ready for an embrace. He charged out the door with a shout of glee, but when he made contact with the unfurled strands of the angel's net, his voice rose into agony.

His skin burst into white flames. Melted from his bones like candle wax. His voice rose in pitch and volume. Inhuman in its suffering.

The net closed around him, and the angel threw the bundle over her shoulder. She turned with her burden, but stopped when she saw Kristophel.

BROTHER

He nodded in greeting.

The angel paused a moment longer before spreading her glorious wings and taking flight. She fled existence in a burst of light, and the crack of discharged power hit Mickayla in the chest.

She fell back into her chair. Cried into her hands until she ran out of energy. She lifted her head to find both Mickayla and Kristophel watching her. "What was that shit?" she demanded.

"That was a Tracker," Amanda said. "They usher the righteous into the circled arms of our Lord and Savior."

Mickayla pointed out into the hallway. "He was fucking screaming!"

Kristophel tipped his head. "He wasn't righteous."

Mickayla sat up. "So where do they take the ones ... the ones like *him*?"

Amanda looked at with scorn. "Come now, darling. Fairy dust is only used for one thing."

Mickayla didn't want to ask. "What's it for?"

"It drugs children into a euphoric state, making them pliable and ... willing. At least you *do* get paid."

Mickayla bent forward to puke, but there was nothing in her stomach. Just a grinding contraction. She sat up and wiped her mouth. The room spun. Sudden exhaustion settled onto her shoulders. She could barely lift her hands.

Her eyelids drooped.

She turned to Kristophel. Pain spiked into her forehead. Opening her mouth to speak took terrible effort. "You never answered me."

He shook his head. "What was the question?"

"Whose corpse was it?"

She imagined she heard Rose's laughter as she fell out of the chair.

Chapter Seven

SHE SAT on the edge of the pier. Leaned back with her hands flat on the gray wood. Her feet dangled just above the water.

This was where Rose usually stepped up behind her, but she didn't feel her footsteps. Only a cold emptiness behind her. Mickayla turned to look over her shoulder.

The white cottage up the hill. The swing set. The jangle and creak of the rusty chains.

Her father sat with the paper open in front of him. The breeze made the corners flap. Her mother walked through the sliding glass doors with a tray. Breakfast.

The morning sun made the glass jug of syrup look like it was full of fire.

Waffles were Rose's favorite. Mickayla liked them okay, but she preferred pancakes. From all the way down by the lake, she couldn't tell which one they were having.

Her mother set the tray down. Shielded her eyes and looked down the hill. Waved at Mickayla, but even from the end of the pier, the worry in her face was visible.

She frowned and lowered her hand. Her father

dropped the paper and brought his gaze to the shore. Neither of her parents were looking at her anymore.

Mickayla followed the line of their gaze. She expected to see Rose running across the wet sand. Splashing into the rippling waves where the silt would churn up by her feet to stain the water black.

What she saw instead was a thin man. Tall and dignified, but old. Gray and narrow. Both hands in front of him, crossed on the handle of a black cane. His pant legs were rolled up. Shoes and socks in a tidy pile safely behind him in the grass.

He looked up from the water. Into her eyes, and his smile was the one that had hung over her in judgement when Kristophel had first spread his wings.

When she had looked up from the floor. On her back and screaming in pain and fear.

Her body had filled with light, and the eyes that floated above her had closed in satisfaction.

The white plaster above her was unbroken. Smooth and clean. Arktis spread his wings into the corners. Mickayla stretched with a yawn as the dream faded.

Amanda's ceiling looked as it always had, she had just never seen it from this angle.

The cushions of the small sofa under the window cradled her from shoulder to toe. Her head rested on the padded arm. The trees swayed in the breeze, and the green leaves rolled and fluttered like dragon scales.

She sat up in confusion. Wasn't it autumn? With the trees all going gold and red? And how could this wall even have a window in it?

Where was the parking lot?

"The fuck is going on?" she asked.

Kristophel sat hunkered over one fist. He brought the

knuckles up to his nose and snorted with his eyes closed. Sat back and smiled. "How do you feel, child?"

Mickayla put her hand on her knees and squared her shoulders. "I gotta admit, I feel pretty good. Maybe not as good as *you* — did you just do a bump of coke?"

Amanda paced through the door trailing smoke over her shoulder. "He is learning many sins lately."

The angel chuckled. "*Revisiting* might be a better way to say it."

"Funny," Mickayla said. "You wouldn't sleep with *me* twice." She pointed at Amanda. "I see you found a cigarette."

Amanda shrugged. "One of the painters smokes."

"So, you went all the way out there? You didn't just snap your fingers?"

"Don't be ugly, darling. None of this is *my* fault. Besides, the workers won't come into my office."

"Afraid they'll get it dirty?"

"No darling. They're afraid you'll touch them."

Mickayla scrubbed her eyes with the heels of her hands. Stood up with a stretch. "I've never felt this good, and it's disgusting."

Amanda smiled. "Living well is its own reward, as they say."

Kristophel laughed at the ceiling. "That means nothing."

Mickayla mocked him with a snort of derision. "Like almost everything *you've* said, it's bullshit."

"I have not lied to you."

"I don't believe you. You're the angel of sin."

"That's not what that means."

"Then define it better. And while you're at it, tell me what the fuck is going on."

He tipped his head in a half shrug. "Very well."

Mickayla rocked back in surprise. "That's it? I just had to ask?"

Amanda ground the cigarette out. "In the short time I have known this ... being, I have come to the conclusion that he is fucking dogshit insane. His plan is ludicrous. His intent is flawed. And he knows he will get his way, because as much as you or I — mostly you, for I know what is at stake — as much as we might protest, we will do as he asks."

Mickayla leaned against the desk. "Whatever happened to free will?"

Kristophel smiled. "Ah, free will. I have a colleague who would be better suited to this argument, but for my part, I do my best to remove it."

Rose would have been better suited to argue. Mickayla stuttered before finding the words. "But ... isn't that wrong?"

"It is. A sin I have committed countless times. It is why I fell."

Mickayla shook her head. "I don't understand."

"It is simple. You will do as I ask, because in spite of free will, I have removed the alternative. You will choose, yes ... but your choice will be what I desire."

Amanda wouldn't meet her gaze. At first, neither would Kristophel. He finally looked up at her, and his eyes shone with unshed tears.

"What have you done?" Mickayla whispered.

"You asked whose corpse it was I carried. It was your sister's."

Mickayla grinned. Wagged her finger like she had caught him in the middle of a practical joke. "Get out of here. I'm still at the doctor's office, right? Like, I never left. Just stroked out on his floor. I mean, come on ..."

Amanda sighed. "I already told you the divine spark

seeks to heal you. All the time. Rolling back the sins. The damage you try to do to yourself. The problems of the body … and the mind."

"The fuck does that mean?"

Amanda slapped her hands on the desk. "Don't you think blaming yourself for your sister's death when you were six years old, and then *talking* to that dead sister for the rest of your life — actually *hearing* her voice in your head — isn't a little … crazy?"

Mickayla shrugged. "Maybe?"

Amanda sighed in disgust. "The remnant is *normalizing* what should be sending you to the fucking looney bin. If nothing else, you'll do what he says, because it will seem *right*. Perhaps not good. Or righteous. But right."

Mickayla threw up her hands. "How?"

"The Sanctum Glorianis," Kristophel said.

"The hell is that?"

"Exactly," Amanda said, as she collapsed back into her chair. "Fucking Hell indeed."

Kristophel looked down at his hands. He held a small black vial. It must have been empty, because he leaned forward and dropped it on the desk with a sigh.

He leaned back and laced his fingers over his belly. "The Sanctum Glorianis is a torturer's academy. Where humans are taught the torments of Hell so they might learn to inflict punishment on those who deserve it."

"Wait a fucking minute," Mickayla said. "You're gonna *torture* me to get what you want?"

Kristophel looked up in confusion. "What? Of course not. Why would you think such a thing?"

Mickayla shrugged. "You haven't exactly been super forthcoming, you know?"

He shook his head. "No, I will not torture you, at least not directly."

"That's not any better."

Amanda held her hand up. "Please. Just tell her what you want."

He looked away. "I already did."

"Kristophel, you are being a wank stain."

He clamped his mouth shut.

"This is bloody ridiculous. I have another hundred years of this nonsense. Being a bloody pimp to damaged women who want to destroy themselves, only to whine about how hard it is." She turned to Mickayla. "It is simple. You will go to the Sanctum Glorianis. You will heal the victims of torture so they can be tortured some more. *Not* so they can continue to suffer, even though never fucking forget that they deserve it. No, you are healing only so you can catch the attention of the headmaster, Tiber Caruso."

Mickayla stared into Amanda's intense gaze. Nodded dumbly. "Okay."

"You are special, Mickayla. You were one soul divided into two beings. The universe tried to right it. *That*'s why your sister died, and not you. An equation that makes one suffer, but you couldn't let go, and she lived on inside you. That's what allows you to carry the divine spark without exploding into a fucking pink cloud."

Mickayla nodded again. "Right."

Amanda lowered her forehead into her hands. "Tiber Caruso is the shell in which Satan has been captured. It is his prison. The headmaster of the Sanctum Glorianis is Lucifer's vessel on earth. Only it is dying, and if that happens, he will be gone, and the balance will shift."

"To heaven, right? Isn't that a good thing?"

Amanda shook her head. "No, because the balance will not shift to Heaven. It will shift to earth, and there are powers here without reckoning."

Kristophel cleared his throat. "It is even more simple than all of that. I removed the part of your soul that gave life to your sister. I took her, and I gave her over to the headmaster. You are to be tested at the Sanctum Glorianis, and if you are found worthy, you will heal *him*."

"Heal Satan?" Mickayla shook her head. "You fucking people are *incredible*. Either that, or I have a better imagination that I thought."

"You will do this," Kristophel continued, "because the headmaster has her, and she will be dragged down into Hell where she will suffer eternal damnation if you don't agree."

"Oh," she said. "I see. I really *don't* have a choice."

"None of us do," Amanda whispered.

Mickayla nodded. Turned away and walked out of the office. Turned right. Down the short hallway next to Room Number Seven.

Rose had always helped with her decisions. Getting her into trouble as much as she had gotten her out of it. This time, she made all the decisions on her own.

Which doorway to walk through. Which direction to go. In a labyrinth that felt like it was deep underground and every window showed a different exterior.

She didn't see a single other person inside the Viazo Grand, and not one locked door.

Who had imagined *this*?

Not her, she was sure of it. She was trapped inside somebody else's dying vision. Maybe it was Rose's. Maybe she was dying again.

Another question to add to the list. Why would God do that?

If her whole reason for being was to heal Satan — a thought so bizarre, it was difficult to complete in her own head — then she was born for it. Manipulated by chance under the excuse of a divine plan.

She was meant to watch her sister die. She was meant to grow up in one fucked-up situation after another. Meant to carve out a little place for her dead sister in her mind. Sharing a soul.

How many others had been born the same, but never found? How many times had God laid the groundwork of an insane angel's mission?

Just scattering these broken people all through time until the Angel of Sin sobered up enough to find her. The intricacies of such a plan boggled her mind. The cruelty of it escaped logic.

She would do anything to bring her sister back. *Anything* to give her sister the life she had been robbed of by a self-centered creator. She would even trade places ...

She turned down a hallway with a set of double doors at the end. Narrow windows showed warm light. She quickened her pace as her decision solidified.

Kristophel was right. She would do whatever he asked — only she needed a little more convincing first.

She threw the doors open and stepped out into the Viazo Grand lobby. Just to the right of the top of the grand staircase.

The ornate ceiling rose up to a height that seemed to defy the dimensions of the hotel's exterior. A great crystal chandelier burning like a suspended star.

The subdued murmur of activity came to an abrupt halt, and she saw people standing in a tableau all around. No angels or demons. Ghosts or goblins. Just people. And they all turned to stare at her.

She kept her chin up. Walked to the stairs, and as she descended she felt like she was in a movie. The star of the show. Every eye on *her*.

The few people that were in her path moved to the side before she could get there. They put several feet between them, as if they didn't want to be touched.

She caught Peterson's eye at the concierge desk. His black face was all shadow and angles, and his eyes narrowed in suspicion, but he didn't say a word as she passed.

The front doors opened, and a breeze at her back ushered her outside. She stepped through into the shade of the covered entrance, and the doors closed behind her. She turned around, and the people had gone back to their business as if she didn't exist.

Maybe even as if she hadn't even been there.

She walked along the front of the hotel and squinted up at the sun. She had parked her car at the rear.

Now she had to go all the way back there to get it. Rose would have said something sarcastic about a journey of a thousand miles or something.

Whatever.

Chapter Eight

THE DRIVE to Hector's Basement seemed much longer without the distraction of cigarettes. Just endless traffic and cool fresh air.

Instead of letting the questions keep rising to the surface, she drove them back under with mindless distraction. She read every billboard. Recited every sign. Hummed along with the music on the radio barely audible over the wind drying the tears on her cheeks.

Rose hadn't just been a voice in her head. She had been a presence. Sounds and aromas. The warmth of skin. The touch of fingers sliding up her arm.

Sometimes, she would glance to the side, and Rose would be there. In the way the dust motes swirled around in a shaft of sunlight. Or a fleeting shadow.

She would even leave, giving Mickayla some privacy. Sure, she would pop up in the bathroom every once in a while. Observe her with a boyfriend, or later with a client. Give her the silent treatment after an argument.

How could a person argue with themselves?

She glanced up at her reflection in the rearview mirror. "I guess you *won't* anymore, kid."

Kid.

That's what she was. Barely an adult. But she never felt like she had been forced into any situation alone. She had always had Rose with her for support. "Forget about those guys." she would say. "You'll be hurt by better than *them* before it's all over."

And somehow, she would be right. She was *always* right.

Mickayla drifted through the years with Rose as her life preserver. Why worry? She would always be there to keep her afloat.

Too bad there was nobody there to do the same for Rose when *she* had died.

Mickayla rolled her eyes. Leaned forward to get a better look at the Hill of Beans sign hanging above the orange and white awning. *This fall, stay grounded with a cup of our Autumn Blend!*

She didn't need Rose to tell her how bad that slogan was. Maybe she didn't need Rose at all anymore.

She laughed as she leaned back. "She was right, though. I *am* a drama queen."

After crawling through a slowdown for five agonizing blocks, she pulled onto the service road that went along the fence and overlooked the shipping yards. Uneven concrete and sinking asphalt patches.

The smell of dead fish, rotten algae, and diesel exhaust swirled into her window to burn her eyes. Soon, it gave way to the beans and wood smoke from Hector's Basement.

Strippers, comics, and singer/songwriters made up the entertainment, but for all of that, Hector's was known for their food. She'd had enough excellent fish tacos Carl brought her to agree.

She thought about how long it had been since she'd eaten. Did she even *need* to eat anymore? *Could* she eat? If it had too much cholesterol in it would the healing spark make her throw it up?

Too much thinking, but there was nothing to read in the back of the buildings next to the dirty boardwalk, except for the *NO PARKING* sign she pulled up to. *NO SMOKING. NO ADMITTANCE.*

Yolks and Jokes. - Every Friday morning!

She didn't see Carl's El Camino. Black and chrome. "It's a '69, not a '70," he always said. "You can tell by the headlights."

She looked down at her watch. There wouldn't be anybody here for another hour at least. Just the sweepers inside to clean up all the stripper glitter and steak sauce. She curled up her lips. If not for Carl, she may have been one of those strippers with A1 dripping from her ass cheeks.

Instead, she got it on with pathetic men old enough to be her father's older brother.

She valued herself far less than those dirty old men so it was worth it.

She laughed as she got out of the Subaru. Wondered what a stranger would think if he saw her. Shaking her head and chuckling to herself.

She walked around to stand between her front bumper and the old ropes stretched between bleached posts. Just the appearance of safety, it would never keep anybody from falling in the filthy water of the bay. Carried out to sea on one of the garbage scows.

Maybe she could look up at the birds as she passed under the Burg-Heartstone Bridge.

She dug through her purse. Rolling the contents back and forth. Laughed at her own frustration when she realized she had been looking for her cigarettes. Her hands still moving out of a habit her brain was in the process of forgetting.

What other pleasure was going to be taken from her?

"Excuse me, are you Mickayla Waters?"

She pulled her purse up to her chest as she turned to face the voice. In spite of the fear that dropped into her guts, she couldn't keep her smile from spreading.

Rose would tell her how much of a weirdo she was later.

The stranger smiled back. A young man. Brown leather jacket over a thin striped sweater. Jeans. Loafers. His hair was swept up in a side part held by product that provided some shine. A satin sheen that moved along the strands as he moved his head.

"Do I know you?" she said.

His smile widened into a grin, and his teeth were perfect, white, and gleaming as if they had just been polished. His blue eyes crinkled at the corners.

He had a nice body as far as she could tell. Chiseled face with smooth skin. Barely an adult. Like her.

She went for older men, but he might have a chance.

"It depends," he said. "Are you Mickayla Waters?"

He wore gloves. Not slick leather that would match his boots and jacket, but rough suede with the fingers cut off.

His presence was suddenly … wrong. Like he had been waiting for her. She slipped her hand inside her open purse. Tried to make it as casual as possible as she felt for the small pair of scissors in the inside pocket, but her fingers found nothing but old tissues crumpled up next to the Zippo.

"I have mace," she blurted.

Blue Eyes glanced down at her purse, then he shook his head and looked up at the bright sky. "I doubt it."

A tattoo peaked out from under the color of his shirt. Vines and thorns. Dark and ornate, it had looked like shadowed stubble at first. Now, she could see it was … something. A symbol or word, but it felt like looking at swarming bees.

She looked down into her purse. Saw the flash of metal but before she could pull the scissors out, another voice spoke from the other side of the car. "It's her, alright. Looks just like what he said."

Another young man. Dressed the same but with red hair. Freckles from eyebrows to upper lips. The same tattoo on his pale skin jumped out like it was in a spotlight.

Blue Eyes sighed. Held out his hands like he was trying to calm down a growling dog. "Look. I gotta be sure. Are you Mickayla Waters? Either tell me, or I'll find out the hard way."

She backed up until her lower back pressed against the rope railing. "It looks like all you got is the hard way."

He laughed and shook his head. "You're right."

He took a step, and she threw one leg over the rope. Ginger lunged for her, but Blue Eyes cut his hand through the air. "Hang on!"

Ginger stopped with skidding feet while Blue Eyes took a slow step to bring him closer.

What was she afraid of? Maybe the divine spark would let her sink to the bottom while they gave up the search when all the bubbles stopped. She would come up hours later covered in fish bile and seaweed. Like Jonah after the whale threw him up on shore.

The image of her splatting her way back to the car made her snicker. Rose would probably tell her to shut the fuck up. Why make things worse?

And that's clearly what she had done. Blue Eyes took advantage of her distraction by covering the last few steps in a single leap. She tried turning into a jump that would take her into the water, but her back foot caught in the rope.

He grabbed two hands full of her jacket and snatched her back. Her purse flew from her hands as she flung her arms out, but there was nothing there to stop her fall. She landed on her back and her head slammed on the ground. Bright light and heat. The sound of a splitting brick.

She couldn't breath. Her hands were claws floating above her, and she couldn't make them come back. She turned her head, and her guts heaved. Nothing came out but a string of bitter spit that trailed down her cheek.

A whooping breath, and the spit drew into her lungs. The cough felt like it was tearing her breastbone apart. She rolled onto her stomach and struggled to her hands and knees.

Jumbled voices behind her. They became more detailed as she caught her breath. "Her driver's license says we got the right girl."

That was Ginger.

"Jesus, she's fucking hot," said Blue Eyes.

"What are we supposed to do with her?"

"He just said to get rid of her."

"What, no fun first?"

"He didn't say anything about that."

"Then let's take her back to the garage."

"Yeah, okay. Let's toss her in the back of the Beemer. You take *her* car."

Mickayla heard the jangle of keys. Who threw them and who caught them? She hadn't been able to keep track.

Steps shuffled closer. She saw a hand coming for her out of the corner of her eye.

She didn't have her keys. The little scissor. The mace she had lied about. Nothing but her fingernails.

She spun under the reaching hand. Brought her clawed fingers up in a blind swipe. She shouted wordless defiance as her blow connected, and Blue Eyes' head whipped back with a trail of blood arching away from the slash that appeared on the side of his face.

Between eye blinks, the cuts were gone. She felt a bit of the spark go out of her. An exhausted sigh as she slumped down to fall back on her ass.

Blue Eyes rose up with a shocked gasp. His eyes were wide and staring. "What did you do?"

"The fuck? You alright, man?" Ginger said.

Blue Eyes waved him away. Watched Mickayla as she pushed to her feet with a groan. "What did you do?"

She shrugged. "I healed you."

"Oh … do it again."

She had to admit, it felt good to feel good. He must have had something wrong with him. Something under the surface. She had removed it for him and he wanted more. She shook her head. "You gotta have something wrong with you first. I need something to heal, right?"

She saw the back door to Hector's open, and she almost collapsed with laughter when she saw Carl step through.

Blue Eyes moved forward, blocking her view of the back door. "I said do it, bitch!"

She grinned. "You got it." She reached out as if she was going to grab his hand, but instead, she drove off her back foot and kicked Blue Eyes in the balls as hard as she could.

He came up on his tiptoes with a strangled scream.

"Hey!" Ginger shouted.

She dropped into a crouch, but she didn't get her

hands up in time. Ginger delivered a looping right hook that felt like a hammer against her jaw. Cracking bone and the taste of blood.

"Hey!" That one was Carl, but she couldn't see him. Her field of view was blocked by Ginger's descending form.

She was on her back. His weight on her stomach as he straddled her. His fist back. A blur. His lips peeled back from gnashed teeth.

Alternating blows came down like jolts of electricity. The back of her head ground into the parking lot. Her hands fluttered up to slap against his chest. His breath was hot. Full of spit. He grunted each time he hit her.

She reached through the water, but no matter how far she stretched, she couldn't reach Rose before she was gone. Pulled into the darkness.

She was on her back on the shore. Waves splashing up her legs. Water in her eyes made everything look like shards of light. It didn't matter that she was still alive. Rose was dead. Her twin sister was gone forever.

She looked down at her body in confusion. Instead of water, she was covered in blood. She tried to ask what was going on, but her mouth wouldn't work. Her tongue felt like it was full of sparks.

Carl had one hand in Ginger's hair. The other held the back of his waistband. He heaved, and Ginger took flight. The top of his head hit the driver's side of the Subaru with a hollow *wonk*, and Ginger collapsed in a heap. Carl took a big step and kicked him in the ribs. Leaned over to brace his hands on the window pillar, and he brought his leg back for another go.

Three times, and his boot found a fresh point of contact. His snarl rose in volume. He drew back for another, and Blue Eyes flew in from the side. A knife extended out in front of him disappeared into Carl's side like he had done a magic trick.

He drove his weight in to pin Carl against the door. Drew the dripping knife back for another plunge, but Carl turned under the smaller man's weight like it wasn't there. Drove one arm up in a block. Shot the other one out to grab Blue Eyes by the throat.

The knife fell to the ground, and Blue Eyes grabbed Carl's wrist. Carl dragged Blue Eyes into a turn. Slammed him into the Subaru. The window shattered under his back.

Still holding him by the throat, Carl dipped down to curve a fist up under the right side of Blue Eyes' ribs. Let go with his right hand as Blue Eyes doubled over. Dug his feet in and brought another punch into the other side. Over and over in a solid rhythm, and every time he made contact, the car rocked on its creaking suspension.

Blue Eyes retched to the side, but barely had time to draw a fresh breath before Carl hit him again. A savage bow that lifted Blue Eyes off the ground.

Carl stepped back, and Blue Eyes collapsed with a pathetic groan.

Carl stood with his shoulders heaving as he caught his breath. Put his hand on his side, and when it came away covered in blood, he exploded into motion. A kick that planted the toe of his heavy boot dead center into Blue Eyes' face. Mickayla looked up at Carl to avoid looking at the mess that the other man's face became, and when Carl gave him another kick for good measure, she closed her eyes.

The following silence was broken by grunting and shuffled feet. She peeked through the narrow slits of her eyelids. Carl had Blue Eyes by the pant legs. Dragged him to the edge of the dock. Right where she had been standing. He bent, and with a shout of effort, he lifted the flopping body to his shoulder. Turned and dumped Blue Eyes into the industrial waters of Burg-Winstead Bay.

He limped back to the car where Ginger was twitching back to consciousness. Carl drew his foot back, and Mickayla barely avoided seeing the kick land in Ginger's face.

The same scene as before, and Ginger splashed down to meet his friend.

Carl leaned back. Narrowed his eyes like he was trying to see her through a cloud of fog. His eyes widened in shock, and he broke into a shambling run. Rushed Spanish in his guttural whisper.

He reached out as he crouched, and she drew back in surprise. Crabbed away from him in panic. "Don't touch me!"

He grabbed the front of her jacket. Halted her progress. She resisted the urge to slap his hands away. "No, no, no." She repeated it over and over as he pulled her close. He sat back with her in his arms. Pressed his cheek to hers.

Some of the spark left her, and he hissed in surprise. Drew back to look at her with eyes filled with tears.

She was underwater again. Fading away as he shouted into her face. He was still speaking Spanish, so she gave up.

She was pretty sure he had just killed a couple of guys. For *her*. But she was safe from him. It was herself she had to worry about.

Chapter Nine

THE SIZZLE of rain on the water. A crash of sound that echoed from the rocks on the shore.

Mickayla stood waist-deep in the choppy waves. A flash of lightning lit up the entire sky. The reflection looked like a sheet of fire just under the surface of the lake.

She closed her eyes against all that bright, but she could still see it. Burned into her vision.

A gaze from the beach made her lift her head again. Peer through cracked eyelids. The old man still stood there as before. Pants rolled up to the knee. Cane planted between his feet.

He stood well into the water. The brightening sky showed the cruel pity in his half smile.

She closed her eyes and turned away.

She was lying on a cold surface. Hard and smooth.

Hands worked their way under her. Lifted her up. "Come on, girl," Carl said.

Her jacket slipped from her shoulders. Her shirt came up over her head with her arms flopping in the air as he pulled it loose. His hands at her waistband, and she opened her eyes.

The bathroom in his little house down in Wilshire. "Never go to that neighborhood alone," he always said. "You're only safe there with me."

Steam rolled out from behind the clear vinyl shower curtain. Water pounded into the tub like a lakeside storm.

The muscles in his shoulder bunched and stretched as he bent to slide her jeans down. She stepped out of them at the bottom. Like a child getting ready for bed at the hands of a loving parent.

Had that ever happened to her before?

She couldn't remember. She sniffed at the tears tracking past the corners of her mouth.

Carl stood with his hands on her shoulders. He must have undressed before picking her up.

She had never seen him naked in lighting like this. Harsh and unforgiving.

His face looked like unevenly chipped stone. The wrinkles and crevices in the skin on his hands perpetually stained with grease from poking inside old cars. Now they were full of dry and flaking blood.

His body was that of a much younger man. Speed and strength that belied his age. His entire torso was covered in intricate fading tattoos.

A young woman's face under his collarbone looked up with a hopeful smile. Mickayla wished she knew who it was.

Carl's hand slid down her arm. Grabbed her wrist. Brought her fingers between them to place her hand on his side above his hip bone.

"This is where the blade went in," he said. His rough voice shook. Tears brightened his eyes. "I felt it slide in. Like … a *heat*. It got me bad."

Mickayla nodded. She didn't have the strength to speak. So tired. The spark left her weak and unsteady. Like a guttering candle flame.

He pressed her hand into the skin to feel the hard muscle and bone underneath. "And now it's gone."

Just the blood stain. The rusty streaks that trailed into the creases of skin. Shining blood in his matted pubic hair. Unlike the rest of his hair, it was shot with gray.

He lifted her hand to his lips. "And now *everything's* gone." His face collapsed into raw emotion. A feeling expressed in tears and bared teeth. Pain and joy.

He dropped her hand and leaned forward. Pressed his cheek to the top of her head. Cried into her hair.

Deep wailing sobs that tore at her heart. This hardcore fighter. This man of violence.

She held him. Pressed into him like she was trying to sink into his skin. She felt her memories of Rose slip a little farther away.

In the shower, they washed the blood from each other. His thick fingers so gentle on her face. Wiping away the evidence of the hurt she had suffered behind Hector's Basement.

And the cleaner they became, the more joy there was. The serious depths were unreachable as they lifted each other up with laughter. In his arms looking up at his smile, it was impossible to see the darkness below them.

Their joy turned to passion, and they stumbled to his bed in a wet clinging jumble.

He gave as much as he took, and she couldn't help feeling guilty for experiencing pleasure at a time when she should have been less selfish.

Lucky as always.

She was crying again, and he stopped in concern, but

she shushed him with a smile. Took up his rhythm, and soon they were one.

What sins had she taken from him? What deep shame was now forgiven? She hoped he trusted her enough to tell her, but she also hoped never to hear it.

Much later, he turned to grab the cigarettes from his nightstand. He shook one out and offered to her. She shook her head. Rolled against him and moaned in pleasure just to be next to him, warm and safe. "I quit."

"No shit?" He held them up in front of him. Turned the pack over as if seeing it for the first time. "Me too," he said with a nod. He tossed them aside with a sigh.

She thought she heard a little bit of regret.

She knew she would have to get up soon. Take another shower.

Her hair was a tangled mess. The slick of water had long turned to sweat, but she was comfortable by his side. A moment she hoped to stretch out as long as possible.

But of course, it ended sooner than she wanted.

"What happened?" he asked.

She shrugged against him, but he didn't push. He just waited. Rubbed her shoulder with idle fingers.

She sighed. "Well. I'll tell you."

And she did. From Rose to Kristophel.

She finished with standing behind Hector's Basement, and said, "And then you came and saved my life."

She kissed him on the skin right above his nipple. Pulled her legs out from under the sheet and got up for the shower she had been promising herself.

It was as good as she had hoped.

Not a lot of products in his bathroom. A nice boar's hairbrush she pulled through her wet hair. She curled her lips in disgust at the prospect of putting on her dirty clothes, so she walked out naked.

She retraced their wet footprints into the hallway, and she found him standing in his white boxers in front of a bubbling coffee pot.

He turned, and his smile froze. Fell into an expression she couldn't identify, but one that made her feel uncomfortable.

"Do you have any idea what you are?"

She put her hands on her hips. "That's a weird question."

He shook his head. "No, you don't get it. You look …"

She spread her hands. "Like a drowned rat?"

"What? No. What's a word that means more than beautiful?"

She clenched her teeth together.

He smiled. "You really don't know, do you? How fucking amazing it is to just look at you."

She dropped her gaze to the floor. She suddenly wished she had put on the dirty clothes.

"I'm serious," he said. "The first time I saw you, I thought you was just another rich white girl finally out from under the strict hands of a father that might have loved you a little *too* much, you know? We get 'em here all the time.

"And they get ruined. Poisoned by what they *think* they want, when all they really know is that it's different. But you … I'll be honest, I've taken advantage of my fair share of sheltered young women who look at me as a way to get some of that danger in 'em. But you …"

She didn't want to hear any more. She was nobody. Nothing special. If Rose had been there, she would have agreed.

"When I saw you, I couldn't believe it. How could anybody over there be looking around and *not* see you?

How could you even be there without a hundred fucking guys already trying to get inside you?

"Usually, any girl over eighteen I let in. If their skirt's short enough. If they look at me pretty. But you … I stopped you at the door. And then we talked. I *never* done that before. And then you came home with me.

"I was amazed. How did I get lucky like that? How did an old man with a face like mine end up with a girl like you in his bed? And you looked at me … like you *saw* me. And then I had a fucked-up thought. I thought, if my daughter had lived, it would have been cool if she had been like you."

He looked away and shook his head. "Kind of gross, right?"

She brought her hands to her throat. Shook her head. "No. No, it's actually one of the nicest things anybody's ever said to me."

He pressed his lips together. "And that's a fucking shame. That I'm the one to say something nice to *you*. Somebody so beautiful I don't even have the word for it. Like the way angels would look if they were around … or like a *dream*. Like somebody looked into my head to see the exact thing that would make me love again, and you were that thing. Just showed up."

He wiped his eyes with the back of his hand. Turned to the coffee pot. He blew a loud breath through pursed lips as he filled a cup. Took a noisy slurp.

"You healed me when we first met," he said. "I didn't know it then, but you changed me. And then you did it again today."

"I didn't do anything."

He turned. "But that's the thing. You didn't do anything the first time either. You just said *hi*."

She walked into the kitchen, but he wouldn't look at

her. He kept his attention on his coffee cup. She ducked under his arm and put her hands on his chest. When he finally looked down, she smiled and batted her eyelashes. "Hi."

His laugh was released. Head back and hands wide. She hugged him, and his arm fell across her shoulders to pull her close.

She slid around him to pour herself a cup of coffee. He cleared his throat behind her. "I think you should do it."

She blew across the rim of her cup as she turned. "Do what?"

"Do what Amanda said."

"Yeah, but what Amanda said was fucking crazy."

"But it's just a touch, right?"

She shrugged. "I don't really know how it works, and besides — I can't believe we're even talking about this like it's … normal. I don't know the terms of the deal. Like, six months salvation same as cash?"

"What then?"

She shook her head. "Like, will I get in trouble for healing Satan?"

He laughed. "I see what you mean. It sounds dumb as fuck when you say it out loud."

She shrugged. "Seriously, though. Whether it is for the greater good or whatever, doesn't that seem like a bad thing to do? Like something that would get you thrown out of the prayer circle."

"I don't know … like … I'm different now. I did some bad stuff. *Lots* if bad stuff. I mean, I went to confession and everything. In the eyes of God, you know, I'm clean. But to *me*? I could never forgive myself for some of the shit I was into … and then you took it away. Just like that. It wasn't God's forgiveness that mattered." He paused to cross himself. Kissed his knuckles and lifted his hand in salute to the Lord before continuing. "It was me. I couldn't live with *myself*. And now I can."

She looked down at the slick of oil swirling on the surface of her coffee. "It wasn't me."

"But it *was*. I touched you."

"You don't understand."

"No, *you* don't understand."

She set her cup down too hard, and hot coffee splashed over to scald her fingers. She shook the liquid off with a snarl. "Understand what? What is there to fucking understand? This is all insane!"

Carl spread his hands. "What there is to understand is what you can *do*."

"Do about what?"

He looked at his hand as he set the coffee cup down. Like if he looked away, he would drop it. He crossed his arms. A stance that probably sent fear into the hearts of many a drunk at Hector's Basement. To her, he looked like he was trying to be stern.

A father about to give his daughter a good talking-to.

"I tell you what. There's a little clinic over on Dexter Avenue. A little place for tore-up kids. Burns mostly. Other stuff. *Brown* kids. Kids nobody gives a fuck about. No parents. No money. Just sitting around hoping they heal enough so foster parents won't puke every time they gotta look at 'em."

She nodded. She knew what he was going to say, and it made her want to curl up in shame. Of course she should have been thinking of somebody other than herself.

"Go there with me. Heal them kids first. Do something you can feel good about before doing the other thing."

"*The other thing*. What a way to talk about it, right?"

"What would *you* call it?"

"Okay," she said. "I'll do it."

His grin made his eyes close down to crinkling slits. He rushed forward and took her into his arms. He spun her around, and she buried her face into the crook of his neck.

Fresh tears.

He was laughing while she was crying. She was *always* doing the other thing.

Chapter Ten

By the time Mickayla got home, she needed another shower. The blood staining the front of her shirt had long since dried in a wrinkled pattern that looked like crusty bark.

At her front door she hesitated. She was afraid Kristophel would be there. She wasn't prepared to face him, and she almost turned around. It was the thought of Rose's voice that brought her around. She would have told her to suck it up. Put her big-girl panties on.

She smiled at the memory of a dead sister as imagined by the living one, and she went into her own home with a little less fear.

Thick cigarette smoke made her regret her decision, but when she looked up after closing the door she sighed when she didn't see the coked-out fallen angel sitting on her couch. He would probably have been naked too. Playing Monopoly and giving himself all the railroads.

Amanda sat on the couch instead. Pale. As ethereal as the smoke that trailed from her nose. The morning sun coming through the big window behind her made her look like a star's twinkle frozen in time.

"Darling," she said. Raised one eyebrow after looking her up and down. "Where the fuck have you been?"

Mickayla shrugged. "Church."

Amanda flickered a pointing finger at the blood stain. "That happened at church, did it?"

"Maybe."

Amanda took a long drag. Tapped ashes into the ashtray without looking.

Mickayla kicked her shoes off. Dropped her purse. Let her jacket fall off her shoulders. "Look, I'm gonna take a shower, okay?"

"Are you going to do it?" Amanda asked.

Mickayla pretended not to know what she was talking about. She pointed down the hall toward the bathroom. "Yeah, I said I was gonna. I'll only be a few minutes."

She got two steps out of the room before Amanda's voice brought her to a halt. "What would Rose say, I wonder?"

Mickayla backed up on her toes. Closed her eyes as she stepped into the sun. "Why do you wonder that?"

Amanda took her time lighting another cigarette. "You know, it's only five more years until the millennium. Can you believe that? The year two thousand. Flying cars and the world wide web in every home."

Mickayla dropped to her heels. "Crazy, right?"

"Darling, will you sit down for fuck's sake? Looking up at you is making my neck hurt."

Mickayla nodded. Tiptoed to the armchair she bought out of the Elder-Beerman catalog.

Amanda smiled. "Very good. Now ... let's begin."

"Haven't we already?"

Her smile became a grin of genuine amusement. "If

you only knew." She took a deep breath. "I've already seen the last millennium turn. The rise of Christ's teachings bringing the light to your darkness."

"*My* darkness?"

She tipped her head in a small shrug. "Not yours personally, darling. You humans have been in the dark since you came squealing out of the clay."

Mickayla shook her head in confusion. "Wait. *You* humans. Why not *we* humans?"

Amanda leaned back. "I only look the part."

"So, *you* humans, then. That sounded kinda judgy."

"Let's just say I'm in hiding."

Mickayla didn't want to say that or *anything*. A shower and a nap. Read that new Michael Crichton hardcover where the dinosaurs come back. Instead, she settled back. "Hiding from what?"

"My past," Amanda said. She crossed her legs. "Do you know how special you are?"

Mickayla laughed. "Not the first time I've heard that question recently."

"It's true, though. God created the universe, but He didn't create *everything*."

"That doesn't make any sense."

"It does if you know the rules."

"The rules to what?"

Amanda blew smoke through her smile. "Why, to all of it. The rules to life as you don't know it."

"That's not what the Bible says."

Amanda snorted laughter. "As if you know what the Bible says. As if *anybody* really does. If God is an engineer, then reality is the machine He designed. Every cog and every wheel. All the buttons and knobs and fiddly bits. And it contains everything that will ever be. From the color of your eyes to how a cock tastes."

That seemed a weird thing to create. Amanda nodded as if she had heard Mickayla's thought. "Exactly, darling. It's the machine that defines those things. He built the machine to take care of the nonsense that he doesn't care to. And everybody has it wrong. From Nostradamus to Dionne Warwick."

"What are you talking about?" Mickayla demanded. She leaned forward and planted her elbows on her knees.

"I'm talking about balance, darling. For what else is the machine designed? I'm sure you yourself have asked how God could be so cruel. Why does war exist and such similar piffle. He is as ignorant of the outcome as are we all."

"Who?"

Amanda didn't answer. She only tipped her head down to look at her from under her brow in incredulity. Mickayla threw her hands up. "So what does that have to do with me?"

"I told you. You're special. Put out into the world as a possibility. A person who sacrificed her soul for another."

"I didn't sacrifice *shit*. Rose died when we were six."

"You said she lived on inside you."

"As my fucking imaginary friend."

Amanda leaned forward to match Mickayla's posture. "Wrong. She lived on in you, because you sacrificed your soul to maintain her life."

"How does that even work?"

"How the fuck should I know?"

"Then how can you even say that?"

"Because it's in the Bible, you dumb twat."

Mickayla rubbed the chill from her upper arms. "I never heard anything like that before."

"I just said that nobody understands the real Word. No human has actually read the true Word. So many things that you could never comprehend, and the machine spins along your ignorance so you can never be harmed by what is really out there."

Mickayla held her breath until she was certain Amanda would make her ask. "What's really out there?"

"The truth, darling."

"So what's *my* truth?"

"You are outside of time. The machine cannot see you because you don't have a soul."

"Then how did I give it to Rose?"

"That's *why* you don't have a soul. Jesus Christ, are you that simple? *Many* humans have no soul. They live in the periphery. Unable to truly take part in life. All the girls that work the back rooms of the Viazo Grand are like you. They escape destiny's notice, but it wasn't until Kristophel showed up that I truly understood why you are so different."

Mickayla felt the chill deepen. Cold into her bones. Like she had been pulled from frigid water and left in the evening breeze. "Why am I different?"

Amanda sighed. Stubbed out her cigarette. reached for a fresh one. "Some have their souls taken. Some are born without them. Some sell them. And some have a single soul split between them. Like you and Rose. You sacrificed. You gave your share to another. Willingly. For she had no way of getting into Heaven, as was her reward for dying as a child. You saved her from non-existence. A beautiful act that rang the bell, and the Angel of Sin followed its echo."

Mickayla felt little fingers in hers. Holding so tight. Just not tight enough. "I don't want it."

"You don't want what? The divine spark? The touch of the Christ? Who the fuck would? The scrutiny one would fall under … worshipped and loathed at the same time. In demand until the power finally left you … and they could still see you."

"Who?"

Amanda sniffed and looked away. "Well, perhaps not you."

"Is that why I can't touch you?"

"Like I said. I'm hiding. Even if forgiveness mattered more than a hog's bollocks, it's the light that would shine upon me." She spread her hands and looked up as if beseeching Heaven. "My sins laid bare in the contrast of absolution, and I would pay. Going to Hell of one's accord, and being dragged there by a Tracker, are two very different things."

"What's the difference?"

Amanda lowered her arms. "A hero's welcome or a villain's reckoning. Which would you choose?"

Mickayla nodded as if she understood. "I'd pick the shaving ads and all that pussy."

Amanda barked laughter. "Precisely."

"So what am I supposed to do?"

"You're supposed to choose, darling."

"Choose to cure Satan?"

Amanda lowered her head. "No, to *heal* him."

"The fuck's the fucking difference?"

Amanda shrugged. "You're not a doctor."

Mickayla couldn't help herself. Laughter spilled out in a helpless gale. She howled it into the ceiling, only stopping when she ran out of breath. She wiped her tears away to see Amanda sitting with a satisfied smile.

Mickayla smoothed her stiffened shirt. Sat back and crossed her legs in an imitation of Amanda's regal calm. "If I choose not to do it?"

Amanda inclined her head. "And that is certainly a possibility. And though Kristophel alluded to it, he did not come right out and say it. Probably why the drunken coward isn't here."

Mickayla's gut roiled in sudden fear. "What do you mean?"

"Simply this, darling. He has given Rose over to the Dark Lord, and she will be pulled into Hell to suffer in your stead if you choose *not* to."

"Wait, what?"

Amanda sighed. Stubbed a third cigarette out, but she paused before grabbing another. "Rose was as real as you or me. In fact, she was more real than you, for she had a soul where you did not. He pulled that soul from your body. You even saw your sister's corpse in his arms, though I'm sure the spark is making you deny the memory."

Mickayla closed her eyes. Tried to concentrate through the confusion. "I don't … how is the spark making me do anything? Or *think* anything?"

"Ah, look at the question you asked. Not one about your sister, but one about you."

"I don't understand."

"I know, darling. The spark has a purpose. That purpose will be fulfilled. If not on the Dark Lord then on somebody else, but you see … failure dooms all of mankind. Not *me*. I could give a shit about mankind, but there is a vested interest in the subject up in Heaven, you see."

"No. I fucking don't."

"Heal Satan, and the machine balances. Humans go on making more humans. God goes on doing … whatever the fuck He does. You however, will die. There is no Heaven for you, as you gave up that option along with your soul, but there is no Hell either, so there's that."

Mickayla felt the little fingers slip from her grasp. Saw the shadow of her sister's face fade into the depths of the churning water. She suddenly understood. Like a sparkle of light seen from under the surface. "But Rose can go?"

Amanda grinned, and her shoulder sagged in relief. "Yes, darling. Rose is the one with the soul. Held by the Dark Lord as a lure for even the *possibility* that you might be the one."

"And if I do it, she will go to Heaven?"

"Yes."

Mickayla wiped her nose on the back of her hand. "How?"

"You have but to touch him at the right moment."

"Okay."

"Well, it's not that easy, darling."

Mickayla pushed back into the chair. "What the fuck? Then what am I supposed to do?"

"You will go to his school, and you will pass his test, and then there will be an opportunist."

"What is the test?"

Amanda shrugged, but her gaze flicked to the side in avoidance. "Only the Father of Lies knows that ... and as his name might suggest ..."

"Fine," Mickayla said.

"Fine what?"

Mickayla nodded as she stood. She avoided meeting Amanda's gaze as she walked by. "I'll do it, but I need a shower first."

"Of course. Kristophel will come for you soon."

Mickayla slammed the door to the bathroom, and with the water running she couldn't hear if Amanda did the same on her way out.

Chapter Eleven

EVEN THOUGH KRISTOPHEL came for her like Amanda said, Mickayla still had to drive. For almost eight hours, he loomed next to her in sullen silence.

She tried to get him to talk. "So Satan lives in Cleveland, huh? Kind of an obvious hiding place, isn't it?"

After several attempts with nothing but the big angel staring out the windshield, she gave up with a shrug. Put a Sting CD in the radio and drove. Determined not to stop for anything other than gas unless he asked her to.

The first stop was for a fill-up and a cup of coffee. He stayed in the car. Still no words from him when they stopped the second time, but at least he got out.

Just before crossing over into Ohio, she pulled up at a One Stop Gas-n-Shop. More gas and a stretch. A satisfying pee, and she was back in the car waiting when he burst out of the front door.

His giant arms were full. Crinkling potato chip bags crushed to his chest. A red licorice rope trailing behind him over his shoulder. He jogged in a fluid crouch with one hand held slightly forward to keep the huge bucket of blue Slurpee from tipping over.

He fumbled with the door handle. Dropped a cascade of snacks. Dribbled frozen blue sugar on the window. A car pulled into the next pump, and his efforts doubled. She could hear his voice growing from a hissing whisper into a repeated grumble.

"Fuck fuck fuck fuck …"

He finally made it inside. Stuffed his haul into the space between his feet. Leaned out with a grunt to pick up what had fallen during his frantic entrance. A Chick-O-Stick.

"Drive," he said as he slammed the door. Took a long pull from the straw. His wide-eyed gaze was focused a hundred yards down the road.

Mickayla leaned forward to see around him, but nobody was coming out of the front door of the gas station. Nobody shaking their fists in the air or waving a gun around. She leaned back and looked at his intent face. "Did you kill anybody?"

He glanced over in irritation. "No. Drive."

She started the car, but she didn't put it in gear. "What did you do?"

He pointed out the windshield. "Go."

"You stole all that junk food and what … knocked the clerk out or something?"

He turned to face her, and his eyes lit with golden fire. "I put the fear of God into him."

She pulled her gaze away and put the shifter into *DRIVE*. Pulled out faster than she had intended. The front tires chirped off the asphalt as they shot into the street.

The slurp from his straw as he got to the bottom of his drink made her release the breath she had been holding. Spots swam in front of her eyes while she hyperventilated.

"I didn't kill him," Kristophel said. "I've known that sin for far too long already."

He spent the rest of the drive in silence except for the sound of his methodical snacking, and the occasional barked directions. "Take the next exit. Turn right, then two blocks up, do a U-turn."

"U-turns are illegal in Ohio."

Silence.

Hours of convoluted turns in an unfamiliar city, and by the time he had her slow down as they entered an old neighborhood, her fingers were cramping on the wheel. Tight muscles in her lower back threatened to spasm.

Her skin felt dry and greasy at the same time. Her hair was lank hunks hanging in her face.

The sun was hitting the horizon when he pointed into a driveway hidden between two falls of ivy at the opening in a stone wall that seemed to grow out of the ground. She shook her head in confusion. The wall appeared to run into the distance to fade before the horizon. She was certain they were facing north. "The wall looks like it's longer than Lake Erie. Like it should be in fucking Canada."

Kristophel shook his head. "It does not go to Canada."

"Then where's it go?"

"Nowhere."

She rolled her eyes. "You're so informative."

She turned into the drive before he could respond, and the air inside the Subaru cooled. Then froze.

"Holy shit." She turned the vents to the red. The fans to high. Her breath plumed out like smoke. The windows fogged over. She ducked down to steer through the hole growing above the defrost vents in the dashboard.

Kristophel rubbed the window with the heel of his

hand to reveal a clear circle. "Perhaps a result of the lake effect?"

Her foot almost slipped off the accelerator in surprise. She glanced over. "Was that a joke?"

He shrugged, and his lips twitched in a suppressed smile. She turned back to the widening patch of clear glass and shook her head in wonder.

They crested a gentle hill, and a square of gray formed in the distance. Squat and dark, it formed into a building as they neared. Arched doors and windows. Tiled roof. Leafless trees and brown hedges.

A wide staircase led up into the shadows of a covered entryway. The driveway led right to the bottom of the stairs.

"We are here," Kristophel said.

"Here where?"

"Stop at the end."

"No fucking shit. Unless you want me to drive right into the foyer."

"I do not."

A few feet before the bottom step, she stomped on the brake, and the car skidded the last few feet on the decorative gravel. Kristophel lurched forward with a grunt but he didn't acknowledge the sudden stop.

She slammed the shifter into *PARK*. Turned the engine off. Snatched the keys out and sat with her hands in her lap. She looked up at the dark eaves of the roof overhang. The gothic stone. Huge ornate shutters. "So, this is the Gloria Estephanus?"

"The Sanctum Glorianis, yes."

"No appointment necessary?"

"They will allow me."

"The fear of God?"

"Yes."

An excitement bled into her like heat. A near giddy expectation. She felt the flush spread across her face. "Alright Kristaballs. Shall we?"

He reached into the space between his feet and sat up straight with a bag of Fritos in his hand. "Let's."

Rose would have either warned her to turn back or urged her to keep going. As unreliable a conscience as she could be.

The Subaru's suspension squealed when it was relieved of the angel's weight, and Mickayla patted it on the roof. Scraped her palm through the frost. "It's okay, girl. You done good."

Kristophel tore the bag open, and a handful of fried corn chips filled his mouth before he took his first step.

The building loomed above them as they neared, seeming to grow taller so it could lean over them. Like it was rising up to tip itself forward to fall on them in a choking crash of stone and dead ivy. The stairs lengthened under her feet, and long after they should have been to the top, she looked up to find half the steps still ahead of them.

"Good thing I quit smoking."

Kristophel grunted in agreement.

She lifted a finger as if checking off a point. "Exactly. Plus, cardio's more for health than weight loss, right? Better than cocaine and Twizzlers, anyway."

She watched her feet slap down on step after step. Lost count as the sky continued to darken. She looked up to see flames flickering in the windows. Wavy glass panes made it look like the inside was on fire. She was certain it was all designed to look spooky, but her excitement continued unabated.

Everything she had done in her life couldn't compare.

Not because of the angel at her side. Or the Addams Family bullshit in front of her. She had just never been on a true adventure before.

A prick of doubt made her sigh. Of course, there may have been a reason for staying home. You never knew what was lurking in the shadows if you got too far from your door. She smiled to herself. That sounded like something a hobbit would say.

They hit the top of the stairs, and she stumbled as her foot lifted to plant on a step that wasn't there. Kristophel caught her, and when his finger wrapped around her upper arm, her hand went numb.

She caught her balance and pulled her hand free. Her arm burned where he had touched her. "Good Lord, let me fall next time."

He shrugged. Cracked his fist off the door twice. Dug back into the bag of Fritos. She turned to look back, expecting to see her car as a speck a thousand feet down, but there it was. Just a few yards away.

"I'm losing my mind. Again or *still* or … worse, I don't know. This is all nuts."

The front door moaned behind her. Unoiled hinges holding the weight of solid wood. She spun at the sudden noise, and made sure she was shielded behind her new guardian angel.

A harsh woman out of an Old West schoolhouse stepped out with an oil lantern held high. The yellow flame cast bouncing shadows across her face, like the skin was writhing from underneath. "This is private property."

Her voice was smooth and polite, but with a hint of disapproval. Not angry. Just a little disappointed.

Mickayla squinted in confusion, and the woman's features settled into concerned curiosity. Actually, she was quite pretty with an inviting smile, and Mickayla found herself smiling back. She stepped around Kristophel, but his hand came out to spread its fingers across her belly. Pushed her back behind him as he advanced a single pace.

He pulled his other hand from the Fritos bag. Wiped the grease on his pant leg. Lifted his first finger up to point at the woman's throat.

Her brow wrinkled in confusion, and she tipped her head away from the light. As Kristophel took another step, she drew her lips back from a snarl, and the lantern went out with a smoking hiss.

Kristophel placed his finger against the bone under the hollow of her throat, and his entire hand burst into golden light. Like a beam of sun shooting up to bathe the entire sky in morning light, and Mickayla closed her eyes against his painful beauty as he lifted into the air on unfurled wings.

The woman screamed with a fowl voice. Mickayla's head filled with visions of sallow flesh and fetid pools of still water. Mickayla opened her eyes, and through the glare, the woman's head now looked like the chittering face of a lobster.

Her skirts fluttered around her knees like sailcloth as she staggered back, and Kristophel ducked his head and pulled his wings to cross the threshold.

Mickayla felt the earth rumble, as if the foundation protested the angel's entry. She followed on her tiptoes, blinking away the tears from the heat of Kristophel's flame.

YOU SHALL NOT DENY THE BODY OF HIS WORD

The angel's voice radiated out like a pressure wave, and all the light from inside dimmed in his presence.

As the echo of his words faded, so did his light, and Mickayla looked over to see him back in the form of the sinner. He reached into the bag and pulled out another handful of chips. Looked around with his characteristic boredom.

The screeching creature was back to being a terrified woman. Her hand clutched over a smoking burn under her throat. The skin showing through the burned hole was shiny and red. Segmented like the lobster she had lapsed into.

Mickayla got as close to Kristophel as she could without touching him. Stood in his shadow and looked down at the floor.

The woman's voice shook in a raspy whisper. "You are not welcome here, but I will not stop you."

Kristophel crunched through the mouthful. Shrugged with one shoulder. "We both know you have not the power to stop me."

Lobster Marm snorted. "I have the power to stop *her*."

Kristophel stepped aside. Looked back at Mickayla as if seeing her for the first time. "Do you?"

The woman glared at Mickayla, and then her eyes widened. She stepped back with a gasp that sounded like a knife across a sharpening stone. The hand that went to her throat was a glistening red claw. "Sin has brought her hence? The salvation of darkness? The foretold bearer—"

"Alright, alright," Mickayla said. "Can we get on with it?"

Kristophel dug back into his bag. "Suddenly so eager?"

She threw her hands out. "I don't even know what the fuck I'm doing here, but for some reason I'm so excited I'm about to shit my pants. Lobster Marm here can either show us the way or fuck right off."

Kristophel tipped his head in appreciation before turning away. "What say you to that?"

Lobster Marm recovered herself enough to pull her

illusion back on. The polite face of a daycare worker. Kind and open. Skin unlined. Hands back to human color and proportions. "Of course I will lead you down."

She looked away from Kristophel, and when she met Mickayla's gaze, her eyes were as black as oil.

Chapter Twelve

LOBSTER MARM LED them down the main hallway. Doors lined both sides, and as they passed each one, it opened, and a child's head poked out with sleepy-eyed curiosity.

Mickayla kept her gaze on Kristophel's back. Focused on the wide muscles so she couldn't see the faces. She didn't want them seeing her either, but there were no rocks to crawl under.

She waited for Rose to say something smart, but nothing came.

At the end of the hall was an arched opening. A set of carpeted stairs dropped into the darkness. A bright flickering light danced at the bottom. Lobster Marm held her lantern up and regarded them with condescending courtesy. "I'm sure you can find your way from here."

Mickayla wasn't sure of *anything*, but Kristophel descended the stairs with confidence. She hurried to follow. Flinched away from Lobster Marm's hiss.

She collided with Kristophel, but it barely altered his course and speed. Like she was a gentle breeze surging forward. She caught her balance. Calmed herself by falling into step with the angel. Watched his face gain detail as they neared the light.

A soft murmur below her brought her attention to the bottom of the stairs. A crowd's reaction. Like a gathering had seen something interesting. She tipped her head up to his ear to ask if there were a bunch of pervs watching porn down there, but the sight of his jaw muscles clenching and relaxing made her think better of it.

Rose would have told her she had made a wise decision, but her own mental pat on the back would have to do.

Two doorways at the bottom. A path that extended each direction. A dark wooden railing at the edge. She waited for Kristophel to pick which way, and she followed.

She realized it didn't matter when she looked out over the railing. Both hands flew up to cover her mouth. Her teeth clamped down on her scream. Her knees buckled, and she slid down to sit on the floor. She could still see through the balusters, and though she tried to shut out what was in front of them, her eyes wouldn't close.

It was the spark. It was called by what it saw.

A round theater of descending rows. Benches and handrails of polished hardwood. The bright burn of a thousand lanterns filled it with light, and shadows crawled across the ceiling in defiance of the radiance.

Each row was full of spectators. Men and women in formal dress. Leaning forward with manic sweat beading on their foreheads. Black woolen suits and broad white gowns.

At the center was a wooden stage. A teaching platform. Like where a Victorian doctor would demonstrate the latest scientific barbarism.

In the center of the stage was a blood-soaked table. A

flayed man lay on top. Open from throat to groin, he was pulled apart like a dreamcatcher.

His arms were separated at the shoulder, and each one was hanging above him. They trailed thin pulsing cords of flesh covered in gobbets of dripping crimson. His organs dangled from suspended baskets. Connected to their origins with glistening vessels and nerves. She could see his lungs inflate. His heartbeat in a steady rhythm.

A small pile of flesh at the bottom of the table quivered with each exposed breath he took. A small blue mound below it. Two red bulbs on either side. She clamped down even harder when she realized it was his penis. Kidneys and bladder. All in a gruesome pile as if they were torn loose in an afterthought.

"Now children," a voice intoned.

Mickayla looked to the left to see a woman that looked like the lobster marm standing near the edge of the stage. A girl and a boy at her side. Ten years old. Maybe twelve.

White lab coats covered in gore. Heavy rubber boots. Gloves and goggles. Apparently, even Hell had a *safety-first* policy.

Lobster Marm's sister pointed at the man on the table. "You have rendered Mr. Leeson as presented in the Nine Trials." She dropped her hand on the little girl's shoulder. "Your cutwork was very impressive, Charlotta."

The girl beamed with pride.

"And your sedation was superb, Nathan. He barely stirred, even when his nerves were exposed and … stimulated."

The boys' grin matched the girls', and they both looked up with pleasure at the quiet applause. Subdued and respectful. Gloved hands and cane tips striking the floorboards.

The woman held up her hands for silence. Tipped her

head at the crowd's compliance. "Now, for the Revival. Charlotta and Nathan will attempt a healing on Mr. Leeson. And in spite of some … doubt and dissent … we are *very* hopeful. This pairing has shown more potential than any in a hundred years." She held her arms wide and stepped closer to the edge of the stage. "Children, if you please."

Charlotta and Nathan walked through the puddles of blood with little splatting footsteps. Mickayla's memory flashed to a day long ago at the lake. Before Rose had died. Out on the back porch putting on their rain boots as the drizzle saturated the ground. It was going to be some good splashing.

Charlotta and Nathan stopped at Mr. Leeson's head. Charlotta over his right shoulder. Nathan at his left. They took their gloves off. The snap of rubber. They put one hand on the side of his neck. The other went to his forehead. They closed their eyes, and the theater went silent with anticipation.

Mr. Leeson gasped. His lungs fluttered, and his heart jumped into pounding motion. Like a bird was inside it trying to flap its way out.

Blood dripping down the side of the table reversed course. The tangle of stringy tissue stretching to the baskets contracted. The edges of his flayed skin twitched. Lifted and folded. drew in to collect the muscle and bone back into his body.

Mickayla dropped her hands and stared. They were actually reversing the damage to the tortured man. Healing him — and then they weren't.

They stepped back at the same time. Drooping shoulder and panting breath. The crowd leaned forward in a hush.

Mr. Leeson's eyes opened.

He blinked as if coming awake from a deep sleep. His lungs expanded in a deep breath. His face tightened as his eyes focused and widened in shock.

His mouth fell slack in horror. He stared up at his shaking limbs, the fingers opening and closing as he tried to touch himself. Tried to confirm what he could barely see.

Tears flooded his eyes, and his mouth opened in a wail. "My God! Where's the rest of me?"

Charlotta and Nathan looked at each other in panic.

"Where's the rest of me!"

The children looked at Lobster Marm's sister for help, but she hung her head in disappointment. Covered her face with her hands.

"WHERE'S THE REST OF ME!"

Charlotta jumped forward and put her hands back on Mr. Leeson's head. Nathan joined her. They closed their eyes. Gritted their teeth in tense effort.

Mr. Leeson's scream became a groan. A whisper. A snore as he fell back asleep.

The children sagged in relief.

Kristophel pulled Mickayla to her feet. She thought he was going to pull her into his arms, and she was going to let him. Instead, he slammed the half-eaten bag of Fritos into her hands. The sound was like a gunshot in the dead quiet.

Every face turned to look up at them, and she backed up until her back hit the wall. Kristophel took their collective gaze off her when he burst into light. Spread his wings and rose into the air above the gallery. Sweeping thunder and wind. They stared as he descended to the stage, and many of them flinched away from the strength of the glow that had turned the theater into broad daylight.

Kristophel landed on his toes and turned to address the

crowd. Mickayla flinched away from what she knew was coming.

BEHOLD

His voice crashed into the assembly, and they drew back in shock.

THE SPARK HAS FOUND TINDER

He pointed up at her, and the benches creaked as the crowd turned to look.

UNDER HER HAND, THE FURNACE OF HELL WILL BE REKINDLED AND WOE TO THOSE WHO FALL INTO THE FLAMES

Mickayla met his gaze. Spread her hands in a confused shrug. "What?"

MICKAYLA ANN WATERS, YOU HAVE BEEN CALLED

She felt the desire stir in her. The need. Not like a casual touch when some of the spark left her to heal in passing. *This* felt like purpose. Like what she had been waiting for.

But she hesitated.

It wasn't what *she* wanted. It was what the spark wanted. What Kristophel wanted. She could choose.

The excitement that had been growing came crashing down into confusion and doubt. Also not hers.

She could just walk out.

The doubt became panic.

The spark didn't want her to go. It wanted to heal.

Charlotta and Nathan backed away from the angel's light, and Mr. Leeson's eyes opened again. His head shook side to side, and his eyes stretched in fresh horror. This time his scream was wordless agony.

She winced at the sound. Looked down at the floor and shook her head. Blinked her tears away. The memory of Rose's voice was as clear as hearing it over her shoulder.

You gotta do it, kid.

She nodded, and the excitement took hold of her again. She couldn't fly like the big show-off down on the stage. By the time she got to the opening in the railing where the narrow stairs went down through the gallery, she was nearly vibrating with anticipation.

She got to the bottom and stepped up on the stage. Mr. Leeson took another breath and screamed in fresh pain, but his strength was diminished, and his voice broke. Tapered off to a gagging cough.

Mickayla wept as she stretched her hand out. Opened her mind to the spark. Felt it take hold. Lost herself in a flash of light.

She stood barefoot outside the village walls. Crumbling clay bleached white by the sun. The sand was warm and soft between her toes. A fresh breeze from the desert brought the smell of water and dates.

The children mashed them against fired bricks. Collected the paste for spreading on baked wafers.

She smiled at the thought of sitting down to eat roasted lamb covered in date syrup. Perhaps the others would like some too. They could gather and listen, for she had many more lessons to teach them.

Mickayla frowned in confusion. Date syrup?

Desert breezes and clay walls?

Shuffling feet alerted her to somebody's approach. A child ducked into the shadow at the end of the wall. His thin arms held a stick against his side. He planted it next to a twisted foot. Grunted with effort and heaved his other foot in a slow hobble that barely covered any distance while she watched.

The child paused to catch his breath. Saw her standing and watching, and he leaned aside as fear folded his face.

She held up her hands. "Be not afraid, little one. For I am the light."

His fear halted. became a glowing grin, and the breeze blew his dark hair from his forehead. He held his hand out as if it was natural to be with a stranger in such a way, and when she took his hand in hers, his grin of joy became rapture.

He stood on solid legs. His feet were straight and true, and she watched him cry through her own tears, and when the child shouted his praises to his father, she pulled back as her confusion deepened.

She stood on the stage with her hand hanging above Mr. Leeson's head. He was whole. Healed into a being of near perfection as a mortal could be. His face mirrored the worship on the boy's face from her vision, and she couldn't bear to see it any longer.

Kristophel still stood in his glory. A smug smile on his glowing face.

Mr. Leeson sobbed as he sat up. Reached for her in thanks, but she dodged away.

She slammed the Fritos into Kristophel's chest, and at the crumpling contact, he was back to his human form. Bored indifference as he opened the bag and dug in for a handful of crumbs.

She spun away with a snarl of disgust. Walked through the nearest door, and as she stepped through, thunderous applause exploded from the gallery.

She looked down at the bloody footprints she was leaving. Staggered to a halt as a wave of exhaustion swallowed her up.

She lifted her head to find herself sitting on the floor with her knees drawn up. Kristophel bent down to pull her into his arms. Ignored her pitiful attempt to slap his hands away.

As she rose into his embrace, she leaned into his ear. "I'm not doing it. I changed my mind."

His chuckle sounded like rocks in a tumbler. "We shall see."

She passed out with the memory of the child's smile lighting her way into her dreams.

Chapter Thirteen

SHE WOKE up in a dark motel room. The rhythm of passing traffic was like waves crashing into the shore.

Her stomach grumbled as she sat up. She couldn't remember when she had eaten last, but she also couldn't remember the last time she felt hungry.

She looked around for a door that might lead to a bathroom, and her gaze stopped on a note tucked under the edge of the yellowed plastic of the room phone.

The writing was a crazy wavering scrawl. *At Big Dan's for pancakes.* Kristophel had written with so much pressure, the pen had torn through the paper at the top of the A. Jagged holes where the I's dot and the period should have been.

It was a clue to a mystery she didn't give a shit about. She washed her face and ran her damp fingers through her hair. The dark circles under her eyes reminded her of the hollow despair in Mr. Leeson's face. She shook her head and looked away before she could glance up and meet her own gaze.

She walked outside without further investigation, and the note became clear. She stood at the edge of an empty space in a narrow parking lot that was parallel to the freeway. Her Subaru took up two spaces in the opposite row under a rusting sign rising above traffic. *THE LAST CHANCE INN.*

"The last chance for what?" she said, but there was nobody around to answer her.

Across several lanes was another sign. Not as high as the motel's. Wide and colorful with a vintage flair. *BIG DAN'S HOUSE OF PANCAKES.*

Mystery solved.

Her keys weren't in her pocket, and the room door had locked behind her. She cursed under her breath. Scrubbed her eyes with the heels of her hands before stepping off with a resigned sigh. She'd have to walk across six lanes and a wide stretch of wet grass.

Maybe a semi would blast her before she got to Big Dan's. A fresher pancake than the restaurant could ever offer.

The small gravel crunched under her sneakers as she got to the edge of the freeway, and the traffic opened up as if her crossing had been planned. Maybe it had been.

Rose wasn't talking, but neither was Jesus, so she just had to satisfy herself with a shrug.

The exhaust fumes were mixed with a spike of fish and algae. Like when they had driven up to the lake and she had hung her head from the window. Passing traffic and the faint smell of the water. Only the aroma this morning was a hundred times worse than the pleasant memory of catching hints through the trees.

Traffic resumed behind her like somebody turned the faucet back on, and she jogged across the diner's parking lot. Most of the spaces had vehicles in them, and a row of big rigs in the back told her Big Dan's was popular. Good food or cheap prices.

She'd find out soon enough.

The front door opened with a grinding squeal. The smell of butter and bacon washed over her, and her stomach growled again. A bubbling buzz of vibration that rose into her throat. A waitress with a Big Dan's t-shirt stretched across her flat chest bopped up with a gum-chewing grin. "You by yourself, sweetie?" Her name was written on a tag pinned to her sleeve. *Deb*.

Mickayla hesitated, then returned the grin. "No, I'm with someone. Big brown guy with long hair."

Deb put her hand over her heart and looked up with her mouth hanging open. "Oh my."

Mickayla could see the silver dental work in most of Deb's upper teeth.

The waitress leaned forward and rested her open hand on Mickayla's arm. "Sweetie, how lucky can you be?"

Mickayla ducked her head in mock embarrassment. "I'm just blessed, you know."

"I should say." Deb dropped her hand and rose up on her toes. Pointed to the back corner. "There he is."

Mickayla suddenly hated her. The way she looked at Kristophel in fawning lust. The way she chewed her gum. The way she said *sweetie*.

She wondered what Rose would have said about Deb as she walked away without thanking her.

She neared the booth in the corner, and Kristophel looked up. He smiled when he saw her, and she blew out a breath she didn't know she'd been holding.

Three plates on a neat stack sat to his left. A plate loaded with pancakes was in front of him. Two pitchers sat at the edge of the table. One full of syrup. One empty save for the thick slick of maple glistening on the sides.

She slid in across from him and reached for the paper menu poking up from the metal holder next to the salt and pepper. "How's the pancakes?"

He smiled. "All you can eat. This is my thirteenth one."

She looked down at the monochrome pictures of greasy food. "Gluttony is a sin."

"I know," he said with a sigh of pleasure.

A thick waitress wearing a Big Dan's shirt that would have swallowed Deb whole sauntered up. Her face was bored, and she held the coffee pot away from her like she was afraid it would make her dirty. There was no name tag pinned to *her* sleeve. "What can I get you, hon?"

First sweetie, and now *hon*.

Mickayla slid the menu aside. "Bacon, please."

The waitress flipped over a coffee cup. Sloshed hot coffee into it. Sighed like she was disgusted by Mickayla's request. "How many pieces?"

Mickayla leaned back. Smiled and batted her eyelashes. "Seventeen."

The waitress lifted one eyebrow. Nodded as she turned. As she disappeared into the kitchen, Mickayla saw her shaking her head.

"Seventeen pieces of bacon?" Kristophel said.

She lifted the coffee up to blow across it before taking a small sip. "What do you want from me? I'm hungry."

He folded half a dripping pancake into his mouth. Pointed at her with the fork. "Gluttony is a sin."

She threw her head back and laughed. It felt like healing. Shocking and satisfying. Purposeful.

She sighed at the table. Stirred cream into her cooling coffee. "So, we'll see, huh?"

Kristophel pushed a wad of pancake to the side so he could respond. "We will see what?"

"Last night, I said I wasn't gonna do it. You don't seem to believe it, even though you already said I had a choice."

He drew his eyebrows down. "I don't understand. What about your sister?"

Mickayla looked out the window. All those cars. Were they running away or going back? "Did she ever exist? Was she just a mental disease?"

He swallowed. "I must admit to a fair amount of confusion."

"I had some psychological damage from watching my sister die when we were children. It makes sense that my trauma would become a part of me, but the spark fixed it. I'm cured, and now I can see she never really existed."

Kristophel set his fork next to the plate like he was worried the contact would destroy the whole restaurant. "Amanda and I explained your sister, as we explained how I am using her. I have sinned against you."

Mickayla waved his words away. "Assuming any of *this* is real."

The nameless waitress appeared with a plate heaped with steaming bacon. She dropped it, snatching her hand back like it had been burned by dripping grease. A fresh splash of coffee in Mickayla's cup, and she walked away in silence.

Mickayla cocked her thumb at her departure. "Like that shit. Who acts like that in real life? This is a dream or a hallucination. Or a nightmare. Or a bad trip. That lobster bitch and the screamer in that Sherlock Holmes hospital? Classic."

Kristophel leaned back. Dropped his hands in his lap. "You think this is all … a dream?"

"Why not?"

"Because what you have seen has not convinced you? Because it is so fantastical?"

She smiled around a mouthful of bacon. "Now, *that's* a word."

"Yet, even in this dream you have made a choice."

She shrugged. "Free will, right?"

The skin around his eyes tightened. "Bingo." His jaw bulged. "There was only one of us created with free will. All of the other angels cannot choose. They can only obey."

She pointed at him with a strip of greasy fat. "The old *just following orders* thing, right?"

He closed his eyes. "I sin because I must. Because I am created to. Every one I commit puts me further from His sight. If you choose not to do this thing, I will never again feel the warm light of His love. The weight of His arm across my shoulders in comfort."

She rolled her eyes. "And Rose always said *I* was dramatic."

Tears pooled in his lower eyelids. "I have strayed so far from righteousness."

She sniffed. "You gonna do the single tear?"

He shook his head. "Why are you so hateful?"

"Apparently, it's because I *choose* to be."

He stared at her, but it was clear he didn't see her. He wiped his eyes with the backs of his hands, but when he bent back to the rest of his pancakes, the tears flowed anew. He sniffed as he took another huge bite.

She wondered if she should feel bad for what she had said. If he was using her for … what? To save the world? That wasn't so bad.

There was a spark inside her. It needed to be set free. "Fuck this," she said. "You got my keys?"

Without looking, he dug into his pocket. Came out with the leather fob between his first two fingers. The keys jangled as he tossed them across the table. "You're not gonna go all *sacred glory* on me? Rise up for a good smiting?"

He shook his head. Curled over his plate.

She sighed. "Come on. This is all ridiculous. You probably put something in my water back in Room Number Three. Like, this is all your fault."

Cigarette smoke tickled her nose. She pictured Amanda and her new habit, walking into Big Dan's with a trail of wispy blue flowing from her nostrils. She looked over her shoulder, and snorted laughter. "Speak of the devil." Amanda walked toward the table exactly how it had been in her mind.

"And the devil appears," Kristophel whispered.

She spun around and shook her finger at him. "See? I'm dreaming. How else can you explain that shit?"

"It no longer matters."

She crossed her arms. "Come on. Stop being a baby. Unless you're a part of my dream too, then I guess it's *my* job to keep you from acting like a baby. Give us a smile."

"Is that bacon?" Amanda asked.

Mickayla slid the plate to the edge of the table as Amanda sat down next to Kristophel. Then she leaned back to see where her dream was going to take her.

Amanda held the cigarette above her head while she folded a piece of bacon into her mouth. Chewed with her eyes closed. Blew smoke from her nose before swallowing.

She opened her eyes and met Mickayla's gaze. "Well, darling. You made an impression."

Mickayla shrugged. "Don't care."

Amanda tipped her head. "I'm sorry?"

Mickayla put her hands flat on the table. "I. Don't. Care. What are you doing here, anyway? Don't you have hookers to pimp?"

Amanda leaned back, and her face pinched in confusion. "I am here at Kristophel's behest."

"Just doing what you're told huh?"

Amanda looked from Mickayla to the angel's silence and back. "What is going on here?"

Mickayla lifted her car keys. "I told you before I wasn't going to do it. So I'm gonna go now."

Amanda shook her head. "No ... no, you said you *would* do it. In your apartment. You said so."

"I saw some shit that made me change my mind."

Kristophel looked up. "I thought this was all a dream."

Mickayla smiled. "Fuck you."

Amanda gasped. "How dare you—"

"Oh, come off it, Amanda. What am I worth? What have I *ever* been worth to you?"

"You are just arguing with yourself," Kristophel said.

Mickayla looked up at the ceiling. "I'm so sick of this shit. So sick of you. I wish I would just die already."

"That just might happen," Amanda said.

Mickayla laughed. "What is that? A threat? I'm threatening myself?"

Amanda ground her cigarette out in the sticky syrup residue on the edge of Kristophel's plate. "What about the gentlemen at the club?"

"What about them?"

"Whoever sent them might send more."

"More what? And how do you even know about them?"

Amanda lit a fresh cigarette. She blew smoke up at the ceiling. "I have friends in low places."

Mickayla spread her hands. "What, like the concierge in Hell?"

Amanda shook her head. "No. I spoke with Carl."

Mickayla waved the drifting smoke away. "Sure you did. You know what? I'm done. I am so fucking *over* this."

"They knew your name."

Mickayla pointed to Kristophel. "So did he."

"That's hardly the same thing, darling."

Mickayla slid out of the booth. "I told you. I'm leaving."

"But the headmaster wants to see you."

Mickayla leaned down to make her face level with Amanda's. "The *headmaster*. Give me a break. Why not just call him what he is? Satan."

"You are making a scene."

Mickayla stood up straight. "So what?"

Kristophel pushed his plate away. "Go, then."

Mickayla shook her head. "Don't tell me to go. I'll fucking choose for myself. I don't need a man to tell me what to do."

"Darling, please," Amanda said.

Mickayla felt her annoyance growing into anger, but she couldn't decide who to aim it at. Them or herself. "Don't," she shouted. "I don't need a *woman* to tell me what to do, either. Or whatever the fuck you are."

Before they could say anything more, she walked away. By the time she got to the front door, she was running. Through the parking lot and straight into the freeway.

As before, there was a gap in the traffic. She thought of Moses parting the Red Sea. Almost looked over her shoulder for the Romans.

She made it to her car. Fell into the driver's seat, and when she slammed the door, the backseat's door glass crumbled in. She'd have to deal with the wind blowing in the whole way home.

It was almost an hour before she realized she couldn't smell the lake anymore, but the aroma clung to her like a fading dream. Like the sound of Rose's scream when she fell into the water.

Mickayla was sick of crying. It was becoming her natural state. If this was a dream, and she *knew* it, couldn't she do something about it?

The spark wanted to heal. It *needed* to make people better. Why not pick somebody who deserved it?

Chapter Fourteen

THE DRIVE back to Burg City was a bleary-eyed drag. She looked up as she descended into the ghetto from the J. Moses East Bridge. realized she had no memory of the last few hours. Just a hazy flash of standing at the pump outside of Rockwell.

The heat coming out of the dashboard was blasting dry air into her face, but the wind whipping into the carbon from the broken window behind her swirled around her hands. The knuckles were red, but her fingertips were blue.

How long had she been asleep? Was she even awake right now? She figured if it was a dream, it might as well be a good one.

She drove into the neighborhood Carl had told her never to come to alone. The sun hid behind the downtown buildings hanging over the small houses like the city was trying to keep them out of the light.

Gun stores, pawn shops, and liquor stores. Trash piled into alleys. Weeds withering in the cracks in all the concrete.

This place held the people down that lived in it. She could feel the despair as she drew her shoulders up. She wanted to hide, and she knew if she lived here, she'd never go outside.

She would stand at the front door and shake her head. No use in even trying. Just sit and watch the other people walking by.

What could the spark do in a place like this?

She couldn't tell if it was her question or if it came from deeper inside herself. Not just a random thought about the unfair nature of creation, but a concept put forth by something else.

Something with divine intentions.

She shook her head as she turned down Lightfoot Avenue. Did the spark have enough power to heal everyone in this neighborhood? This city? The world?

She felt a question mark in her head. Like a shrug felt through an embrace.

"Great, now I'm talking to *another* imaginary friend."

The smile she felt reminded her of Rose, and she nodded. Of course it would. The dreamer and the manufacturer of the dream were one and the same.

She parked on the street two houses down. Locked the doors out of habit. Laughed at herself when she looked into the shattered back window.

She felt like a shadow as she walked down the uneven sidewalk. She dragged her fingernails along the rusty chain link fence to her right. Kicked a rock skittering into the street.

A lamp above her head clicked on with a hesitant buzz. A screen door banged open. She looked up, and Carl stood on his front porch. A black man-shaped hole in the doorway. The light behind him looked like a golden aura.

She stopped at the corner of his yard. Looked down at

her feet. His appearance was further proof that she was dreaming. Making it up as she went along.

He was what she needed, and when she thought about him, there he was.

A doubt floated up. A whispered question.

How do you explain the horror show of Mr. Leeson?

That was just … chemicals.

The bloody beating from the two fucks behind Hector's?

A nightmare. Too much valium and wine and nicotine.

"What are you doing here?"

She looked up, and Carl's face looked like a skull. She caught her breath and blinked. His face was just shadowed by the orange street light.

She stepped into him. Tightened her arms around him, and when she felt him pull her against him in return, she sagged in relief.

He was solid and warm. Comforting. A far cry from what she had put herself through a few hours ago. In fact, he was the only good thing in all this. The light in the darkness of the despair created by her dying nightmare.

"How long will it last?" she said.

He pulled her away and looked down into her eyes. "How long will what last?"

"The pain," she whispered.

"Oh, babe. I have no idea. The only thing I know for sure is mine is long gone. Thanks to you."

He pulled her into motion. Walked her to his porch. She looked over her shoulder. Into the darkness down both sides of the street. "Is it always this quiet?"

He followed her gaze. Shook his head and drew his eyebrows down. "No. It's been weird. Even down at Hector's. Like everybody's waiting for something."

"Everybody who?"

He shrugged. "Like the whole *city*."

She dropped into one of the wooden rockers next to the door. He had found them in the trash outside of the old Kmart. A little glue and a couple of clamps, and they were good as new. He was proud of his handiwork, but every time she sat in one, it creaked and moaned underneath her.

He leaned against the post that held the porch roof up. She looked up at him as she rocked. "What do you think it's waiting for?"

He looked down and crossed his arms. "You want me to tell you what I really think?"

"Yes, please."

He shrugged with one shoulder. "I think it's waiting for *you*."

She sighed and tipped her head back. "That's what I was afraid you'd say."

"I think it's true."

She leaned her head back. "Yeah, well, what it really means, is I must think it's true too."

"What does that mean?"

"It means our dreams are what we make of them."

"That doesn't really help me understand."

She smiled. "I know."

The runners squeaked as she rocked. Like the porch's heartbeat. He let her sit in silence for a brief time, but just as she was ready to ask him what was next, she heard him shift his weight off the post. "So what do you want to do?" he asked.

She looked at him through the slits of her half-open eyelids. "I want to do something *good*. And I realize it's what I've *always* wanted."

"What about me?"

"I already did *you* good."

"That's not what I meant."

She opened her eyes all the way and stilled the rocker. "Then what do you mean?"

"I want to do something good too."

She nodded in understanding. "So what do we do?"

He looked away. Like a shy boy trying to get up the courage to ask her to dance. It was sweet and sexy, and she would have given up every good deed if he had suggested they go to bed.

"Remember those kids?" he said.

She smiled. That would work too. "Yes, I remember."

"You wanna go?"

"What, right now?"

He nodded and stuffed his hands into his pockets. "Why not?"

"I don't know. It's kind of late, isn't it?"

He smiled back. "Nah. It's barely past five."

She looked down at her wrist in shock, but she wasn't wearing a watch. Couldn't remember the last time she had cared what time it was.

She held her hand out, and he took it to pull her to her feet. They were grinning like fools, and she felt a calm joy. A warmth of pleasant anticipation. She thought it was hers, but it felt so good it didn't really matter. "Let's go," she said.

He nodded and kept her hand in his as he stepped off the porch. Led her to the sidewalk.

She glanced at his El Camino as they passed it. "We're walking?"

"Sure, It's only a couple blocks, and nobody's gonna fuck with me here. Why, you cold or something?"

She pulled her jacket closed with her other hand. "No, I just didn't realize it was so close. And I have no doubt about my safety."

"Yeah. I grew up here." He cocked his thumb to point behind him. "That was my grandma's. She never let us speak Spanish there. Said we needed to fit in better."

Mickayla laughed before she could stop it. Clapped her hand over her mouth. "I'm sorry, it's just you kind of stand out."

He smiled and pulled her under his arm. "But not then. I was always real small until high school, then I blew up. Then I got mean. *Real* mean. Ain't a gang in this town I ain't fucked with. But even then, I got most of my tattoos in prison. I seen every sign and tag come through Twyker Island before they shut it down. And I ain't never seen tattoos like them ones those dudes had on their necks."

The sudden change in conversation jolted her. She shook her head and pretended not to understand what he was saying. "What dudes?"

He snorted in disbelief. "The ones that tried to kill you. With the thorns and shit tattooed over their throat. Didn't Amanda tell you? I talked to her yesterday."

Yesterday. Last night. This morning. It was all a melded block of time that had no meaning. Like how the days passed in a dream. Slowed to a crawl in a nightmare. Jumped from moment to moment with no sweep of the second hand.

She leaned her head into his chest. "She told me. I just … forgot."

"Uh huh," he said. Incredulous and hesitant, but he seemed to let it go.

He pushed her into a right turn, and she looked up at a wide and low building. Like it was trying to bury itself on the corner. An abandoned lot to the left looked like negative space. Looking into its shadowy depths made her think of dark eyes.

The bottom of a lake.

"What's this?"

He swept his hand toward the building like he was a tour guide. "St. Miriam's Clinic."

The building was so plain. Just a small placard with the address next to the front door. "But there's no signs or anything."

"Yeah. It used to be a female clinic. They did abortions and sex ed and stuff. There were some people from uptown that didn't agree with what was happening inside, and back in the early eighties, they tried to burn it down. Ever since, the clinic decided it was better to not advertise."

And she was supposed to believe in God. She shook her head. "Do they have electricity?"

"What?" He looked down at her in confusion, then he grinned. "No, the windows are blacked out with these … like, indoor shutters. They take their shit serious."

He led her to the front door. "It's never locked, though. Open to all who know about it. Funded by a bunch of churches and a lot of the people in this neighborhood. We're good people, you know."

The door opened, and they were bathed in warm light. Quiet music and laughter. Like a portal had been carved into reality, and on the other side was a normal world. One where she never had to doubt the existence of a higher power.

"Sister Wanda," Carl shouted, and he left Mickayla behind as he rushed forward. The door closed on a pneumatic hinge with a sigh that sounded like it was tired of holding the outside world at bay.

A small nun stood from a desk, papers and pen dangling from her hands. "Carl Iglesias," she cried. "We can't get rid of you, can we?"

She squealed in delight when he scooped her up and spun her around. He dropped her back on her feet, and she stepped back to look up at him. "Sister Lucinda said you were here just yesterday. Oh …" She saw Mickayla and took a step back. "Excuse me, but who is your lovely friend?"

Carl jumped the space between them and grabbed Mickayla's hand. "This is a friend of mine."

Sister Wanda nodded. "As I gathered. *And* as I said."

Carl grinned and ducked his head. "Right. Her name is Mickayla Waters." He leaned in to whisper into Mickayla's ear. "She practically raised me through middle school when my grandma got sick. I'm always nervous around her."

Sister Wanda flapped her hands, and the papers crackled. "That's nonsense. I'm just little ol' me."

Mickayla looked closer. The woman's face was older than it first appeared, but still not old enough to have been around a developing Carl Iglesias. Mickayla shook her head. "Maybe you went to school *with* him, but there's no way you're old enough to have been his what? Teacher?"

Sister Wanda grinned. "Bless you, Mickayla. That's very nice, but my joints would argue with you." She turned back to Carl. "It's almost dinnertime. We're about to bring the carts into the ward."

She tilted her head toward the wall behind them. Mickayla turned to look at what the nun indicated. It was a wide observation window set into the wall. It looked into a bright room lined with hospital beds.

The children Carl had mentioned were there, and Mickayla gasped in shock. Her hands went to her throat as she stepped toward the glass. Her reflection was a ghost.

Bandages, scars, and twisted limbs. These children were in need of medicine they couldn't afford, and by the looks of some of them, the medicine didn't exist that could cure them.

The sight of them turned into a blur of color and movement as her eyes filled with tears. Carl and Sister Wanda were nothing but shaded blobs behind her.

She closed her eyes, but she could still see them. The children, and in spite of their misery, she could still hear the laughter. The small sounds of joy the other sisters were able to coax from such sadness.

Her feet slid into motion to carry her to her right. Her hand reached out on its own, and a cool doorknob was under her fingers.

A woman's voice behind her rose in alarm. A man's voice spoke out to meet it, and Mickayla turned the knob.

The door opened, and she stood on the shore of a river. A warm breeze blew her robes into a flutter around her legs. A young man with his cheeks dark with a curly beard knelt in front of her. Slid one of her sandals off. Then the other.

The young man … Peter, that was his name … scooped water into his hands. Splashed her feet and rubbed the dust from her skin. She was proud of the lesson he had learned. Refusing to wash her feet had been a simple defiance born of embarrassment.

She was no better than any of them.

Peter finished. Stood with a humble nod and backed into the water to join the others. Her disciples. The villagers in need of healing of body and mind. Those in need of spiritual enlightenment and fulfillment.

Those people sick in their souls. Awaiting her light.

She shook her head in a moment of doubt and confusion. Where was she? What was this river? Who were these people waiting for her? But when she looked up to see them standing in the clear water — their faces lifted to the sky, open and joyful — she couldn't help but smile.

The doubt fled as she stepped in to join them, and she

touched all that needed it, and when she climbed out on the other side, they were all clean and whole. Healed of ills and evil.

Some of the spark had left. With the same pleasure of release as always, and she worried that it was too diminished, for there was so much more to do in the world before the end.

Mickayla stood in the center of a throng of children. They sat at her feet. Looked up at her with open mouths and crying eyes. The sister sat among them. Praying hands and uplifted faces.

Sister Wanda clung to Carl's side. Digging her fingers into his shirt. Staring at the children in disbelief.

Mickayla closed her eyes and shook her head. If Rose had ever been there, she would have said, "Like these people have never seen a miracle before."

Mickayla fell forward in a faint. The river closed over her head, and she sank to the bottom.

Chapter Fifteen

HER LIFE WAS BECOMING a series of awakenings. One of these times, she would either never wake up, or wake up for the last time … only to realize it had all been a dream. Then she would die.

"So I guess both would be the last time, then," she said through a yawn as she stretched.

Plain white ceiling above her. Rough fabric under her hands. She sat up. Froze when she found a wide-eyed nun watching her. Mickayla waved. "Hi."

The nun sipped in a small gasp, and her hand rose to her chest like she was feeling for her heartbeat. "Hi."

Mickayla nodded. "Yep. That's how it works. I'm Mickayla."

The nun mimicked her nod but she didn't smile. "Janice."

Mickayla waited for more but ended up sighing into the silence. "So … what's up?"

The door behind the nun opened, and Sister Wanda rushed in with a coffee cup held out in front of her. Her cheeks were ruddy. Eyes bright and focused. She offered the cup to Mickayla. She avoided making contact with her fingers. Stepped back to watch her take a sip.

Hot coffee. Strong, black, and full of tequila. Mickayla tipped her head in a mock wince. "Whoo, was that Carl's idea?"

"No, dear," Sister Wanda said. "That was mine."

Mickayla lifted the cup in a toast. "I like it."

"We all do from time to time." Sister Wanda turned to the other nun. "Sister Janice, if you please. The children still need their sleep ... if any of us will manage to sleep for a while."

Sister Janice nodded. Rushed for the door, but before walking through, she glanced back at Mickayla. Raised her hand in a silent goodbye, then disappeared into the hallway.

"She acts like I'm Freddy Krueger," Mickayla said.

Sister Wanda sat at the other end of the couch with a groaning sigh. "You must forgive her, dear. You are not something a person can prepare for. Just a prayer away."

Mickayla slurped the spiked coffee. "So, now what?"

Sister Wanda put her hands in her lap. "This city is ... a special place."

Mickayla shrugged. "I guess."

The nun continued as if she hadn't heard. "In some ways, it is the most special city in the world. Not in that Burg City Pride you hear all the time, but on something a little more ... meaningful."

Mickayla brought one leg up so she could turn to face her. Look the nun in the eyes. "Is there something you want to say? You act like I'm not going to believe you, but I assure you, as this is my dream, I'll have no choice. In a way, I guess I never did."

Sister Wanda's eyes narrowed. "The mayor's family has one of the oldest names on the East Coast. Largely responsible for running off the natives and drawing the first maps of this area. And it wasn't to own the land or the minerals or even the *people*. It was to own power."

Mickayla finished the coffee. Cradled the empty cup in her lap. "What kind of power?"

Sister Wanda shrugged. "Ultimate power. And proof of its existence is you."

Mickayla shook her head. "I don't think you understand what's going on."

Sister Wanda held up her hand. "Please. I've spent my life with Christ. Most of it here in the weirdness of Burg City. Where angels and demons walk in the light of day. Where the mayor's family maintains open portals into Hell. Where the dark power of Satan is spreading into every shadow and soul. And then you came along. The answer to a prayer I didn't even know I had spoken out loud."

Tears flowed down her cheeks, and she looked up at the ceiling. Opened her hands palm up as if readying to catch the rain. "These children have been healed by the touch of some holy power, and there are more children in need."

Mickayla leaned forward. The spark inside her jumped and jittered like an excited puppy at his master's return. She closed her eyes and looked inside herself. It felt like standing on the edge of an old quarry that had filled in with clear water. The power left in the spark, and there was no bottom. She could heal every child in the world.

"I have spoken with some others who share my responsibility."

"Other clinics?" Mickayla asked.

140

Sister Wanda smiled as she lowered her head to look at Mickayla. "No, dear. Other guardians. Watchers, really. We observe and report. One young pastor in particular has become a great ally to us here at Saint Miriam's Clinic. He was very keen on you when I called. His name is—"

"Owen," Mickayla said.

Sister Wanda sat up in surprise. "Yes. But of *course* you've met him."

Mickayla shook her head. "He wasn't very keen when he kicked me off of church property."

Sister Wanda put both hands over her heart. "That doesn't sound like the young man I know, but he did mention as much. He asked me to convey his sorrow at his treatment of you. Your dilemma was a little outside what one so young felt capable of handling. I can see how he thought that challenge was too great. He's not part of our church, but he has looked after these children as if they were in his own congregation. One of the few who listened to our pleas. Why, I could almost believe *he* sent you."

Mickayla stood. Leaned to the side to set the cup on the little table at the end of the couch. The spark had settled, and a sweat sprung out on her forehead. She was suddenly uncomfortable at the mention of other people. More eyes on her. More people sitting in judgement over her. She spread her hands. "I don't even know what I like."

Sister Wanda shook her head in confusion. Mickayla held up her hand for a quiet moment. "I mean, everything I like is because somebody *else* likes it. Everywhere I go is because somebody else pointed me in that direction. The things I've done ... I don't see them as bad or good or *anything* really. Just like the ticks of a watch. Just one thing after another until there are no more things left."

Sister Wanda nodded. "I understand, dear."

Mickayla sighed. "That's great, because I sure don't."

"I don't expect anything from you. The only one who can do that is God. And even then, His expectations can only be known in an abstract way. Just do good in the world."

Mickayla crossed her arms. "I want to, Sister. More than you know. I just don't know how."

Sister Wanda nodded. "You need time. To think. Maybe to pray?"

Mickayla shook her head. "I don't pray."

"That's okay, dear. He hears you anyway."

Mickayla laughed. Wiped her eyes as Sister Wanda leaned forward to get momentum to stand. Mickayla rushed forward to help her up, but the nun drew away and held up her hands. "Please, no."

Mickayla froze in confusion until she understood the woman wasn't denying her help. She was denying her touch. The *spark's* touch. "Why?" she asked.

Sister Wanda smiled. "I can't justify removing even a tiny bit of your healing divinity when it could be used on a child in need. Just *one* more child healed is worth more than every painless night I can imagine."

Mickayla stepped back and lowered her hands. She couldn't understand it. She would have elbowed her way to the head of the line. And so would *most* people.

The spark warmed inside her, and she suddenly got it. It wasn't up to *her* to decide who was worthy of healing. It was up to the one being healed. It was acceptance.

Sister Wanda was already gone by the time she looked up from her thoughts. The doorway darkened and Carl stood there. Put one hand on either side and leaned in. "You are so beautiful."

She looked away, and her face felt like it was tight with

a sunburn. "I'm selfish. An unrepentant sinner. Mostly, though, I'm lucky."

"Tell that to them kids."

She looked up and clasped her hands in front of her. "Can we go, please?"

"Go where?"

"I just want a little time to, you know … adjust. Get my head right. A lot's been happening, and there's gonna be a lot more."

"Like more healing? More kids?"

She nodded. "It's the only way I can live with myself. If I can do just one good fucking thing."

He took her into his arms. Forgave her just by being there, and she knew she didn't deserve his love, but nobody else was there, so she took what was offered.

"Is there another door to this place?"

"You wanna go out the back?"

She nodded into his chest, and he pulled her into the hallway.

She hid her eyes against him. Kept her face down as he murmured to Sister Wanda on the way out.

"The children will be disappointed," the old nun said, "but I understand. But you *will* be back?"

"Of course," Carl said.

Mickayla nodded again, and she didn't care if the nuns could see it or not.

He led her into the shadows of the alley behind the clinic. Around the dark building and to the sidewalk bathed with the weak orange light of the failing streetlamps.

"You wanna go to my place? The puppy's okay on her own if you wanna go home instead, though."

She sniffed and wiped her eyes. "It's been a long and

tough couple of days. Can I just go home to get some stuff, then back here so we can be close to the clinic?"

"Sure," he said, and he bent down to kiss the top of her head.

It was where she wanted to be for the rest of her life. Right there under his arm. Children around her feet. She saw the people standing in the river under bright sunlight.

Was it a dream or a vision? A memory?

She dismissed it. Some flicker of something while she had slept. Or while she was in a coma.

Carl led her to the passenger side of his El Camino. Opened the door for her. Formal. Like a gentleman on his first date.

She leaned her head back while he ran around to the driver's side. Unlike her Subaru, his car roared to life with sound and power. She didn't understand his fascination with the machine. Or even share his appreciation.

It didn't even have shoulder restraints.

But *he* loved it. Grinned most of the time he was behind the wheel. She wouldn't mind rising along with him. She closed her eyes to engage in a little fantasy. As his queen in the passenger seat.

The look of love and pride on his face when he looked over at her. She could return in a private moment shared between lovers that had found each other in spite of the pain they had suffered. In spite of the suffering they had caused.

Wouldn't that be an amazing life? She wondered what Rose would have said to that.

"What the fuck?" Carl said.

She sat up like she had been jolted by a surprise electrical current. "What?"

He squinted into the rearview mirror with a snarl.

"Some asshole is riding my bumper with his fucking brights on."

"This city is full of the worst drivers."

He nodded. "The worst people. Lemme slow down a little."

"Why?"

"So they'll pass. Or maybe I'll pull over, you know. I ain't in the mood for no fighting tonight. I don't wanna hurt people anymore."

She knew how he felt, but before she could respond, the car shook with impact.

"Motherfucker!" Carl shouted.

The engine roared. So much for slowing down.

Instead of panic, Mickayla felt a calm settle over her. This was what she should have expected. This was how nightmares worked. Like the hallway that lengthens as you try to run from the monster. The heavy feet that felt like they were set in concrete.

The rug pulled out from under you as you finally got to rest.

Just when she had found a kind of purpose. Learning to appreciate what was inside her. A decision made. It figured.

Maybe she wasn't so lucky after all.

His hands were straining on the wheel. His mouth worked around shouted words, but she couldn't make them out. She could only hear grinding metal and squealing tires. Lights spinning and flashing.

Jarring impact against the guardrail at the entrance to the J. Moses Bridge. Her head snapped forward then back with a crack of lightning inside her neck.

The lap belt held her ass in the seat, but her arms floated up as the El Camino soared into the air.

She thought of the assholes behind Hector's. Their

hideous tattoos. The rage in their eyes. The fists coming at her face over and over.

They found her again.

The car hit the dark water, and her face crashed into the dashboard. Her nose crunched like tempered glass. Her cheekbone cracked like a pine knot in a bonfire. Her skin split. Blood gushed into her eyes and hair.

The horn blared in a warble. Cut out as the dash lights died. Carl was a bloody mess. Lips torn. Nose and teeth crushed into a dark hole in the center of his face.

Water rushed in to cover her feet.

Like in the bottom of an unsteady boat. "Stop it," she shouted at Rose.

Her sister sobbed in fear, and the boat rocked harder. "Rose, stop it!" she screamed.

Her father's voice behind them floated on the wind. "Mickayla! Rose!"

The boat hit something under the water. It tore and scraped along the side, and they spun into a wave. It lapped in to pull them in a list. Water covered her thighs. The cold took her breath away.

The weight of the water took the boat out from under them. She kicked and paddled. Choked on water. Rose clung to her shoulders.

Mickayla slapped her hands on the lap belt. Water sputtered up in a wash of bubbles that smelled like oil and rubber. It covered her chest. Pressed up to her chin. She dug her thumb into the button, and the belt opened.

She bobbed up to the headliner. It was dark. Churning water and rising panic.

She reached over to find Carl's shoulder. Walked her hands down his arm. Took a deep breath and reached to his waist.

Rose tore from her grip. Mickayla flailed her arms.

Found her sister again. Pulled her to her, and they both went under.

She opened his belt. Cried out her remaining air in joy. Shot up to bang her head against the slanting roof. Pulled in a whooping breath. Heard Carl do the same.

She pushed him aside. Slapped her hand on the closed window.

The light above the surface flickered in shuddering flashes. The lights on her father's boat. Lightning. Flashlights. Right where they had fallen below the waves. She wanted to cry out. Her lungs felt like they were full of fire.

The window crank turned easier than she expected. Was it because of Carl's love for the classic car? The care and pride he had taken in its restoration?

Before she could speculate further, a wall of water rushed into the window opening. It pushed her back to hold her against Carl's side.

She took his hand. Pushed against the receding pressure. Cranked the window to the bottom. It felt like somebody was pushing toothpicks into her ears. There was nothing but blackness all around. No way to tell which way was up.

Rose was pulling her. A weight she had no hope to swim against. One of them had to let go. Both of them would die. She felt Rose's fingers loosen, just before somebody grabbed the back of her collar.

Her empty hand thrust into the depths below her as she was lifted to safety. Into the arms of her father. He crushed her head into his shoulder and wept into her hair.

Carl's weight pulled her arm straight. Threatened to slip from her hand. She gritted her teeth and kicked.

Lights flickered above her. Orange and blue and red. Rippling white refracted through the waves.

Her head broke through the surface in a burst of

confused noise. Hands all over her. Pulling her into the boat, but she couldn't see her father's face. Only the faces of strangers looking down at her. She rolled to the side to see if Carl was alright, but he wasn't there.

Her hand was empty. Like Rose, he was gone, and there was no reason for her to be alive again.

Except to be alone.

Chapter Sixteen

HERE SHE WAS. Again waking up in a strange place.

A hospital bed. A sterile room much better appointed than any hospital she had ever been in. Marble tile and wood paneling. Like the older parts of the Viazo Grand.

Her hands were cold. Empty. Like they had recently held something that had slipped away.

No.

She tore her mind away from the memory. Focused on her surroundings instead. There were no beeping machines hooked to her. No IVs. It was all pushed into a silent corner.

The wall next to her was mostly a window. Rolling hills ablaze with the colors of fall, like the forest was on fire. Puffy white clouds instead of rising black smoke. Blue sky above it all.

A beautiful day to start the rest of her life.

The spark was subdued inside her. She couldn't blame it.

The door opened, and a man walked in. Dark balding

hair. Round glasses on a pinched face. He looked down at a clipboard he held up to his nose.

He glanced up and met her eyes. Looked down like he had seen her naked. She looked down, but there was nothing to see but her gowned body under a silk sheet.

"Good morning, Miss Waters," he said. His voice was full of twitchy nerves.

She kept her mouth shut while he made a show of studying whatever was on the clipboard. He nodded to himself and looked up but he set his gaze on the center of her forehead instead of on her eyes. "Do you have any questions?" he asked.

She pressed her head into the pillow and laughed until tears flooded her eyes. "Are you kidding me? How's about where the fuck am I?"

His lips lifted in a greasy smile. Like the muscles were unfamiliar with the movement. "Of course. You are in the Lucius Family Sanitorium."

She nodded. "That actually makes sense. I feel like I'm going crazy."

He sighed. "I said sani-*tor*-ium."

Mickayla stared. He sighed again. "It is for the family's long-term *physical* care."

"What family?"

"The Lucius family, as I already said."

"Okay?"

His gaze dropped to look into her eyes for the first time. "The mayor of Burg City?"

She nodded. "Gotcha."

"Miss, according to your chart, there is absolutely nothing wrong with you, and there is no wonder why, but perhaps you were … injured before?"

"Before what?"

"Before you were touched by the Remnant of Bethsaida."

"You know about that?"

"We all do, yes."

She growled in frustration and threw her sheet back. When she swung her legs from the bed, he jumped away with a squeak of fear. She looked at him in confusion. "You see a mouse or something?"

He swallowed and shook his head. "I am not to touch you."

"What if I touch *you*?"

He backed away. "Please, no."

"Calm down … what's your name?"

"Greyson."

"You a doctor?"

He ducked his head. "Of a sorts."

She stood and walked to the window. "What's going on, Greyson?"

"I have no idea."

Her sigh spread condensation in a jagged circle in front of her face. "How'd I get here?"

"Miss Waters, I can only speak to what happened *after* you arrived."

"Okay, so speak to it."

"You were carefully placed in the state you find yourself in. Apologies, but we were not told of your … ability at first, and there were several of our staff who availed themselves of your touch."

She curled her lips in disgust. "That sounds kind of creepy."

"They have been dealt with, I assure you."

"Why assure *me*? It looks like that's what I'm supposed to do."

"Perhaps you're not supposed to do it to *everyone*."

She turned around and leaned back against the window sill. "I keep getting little lectures about free will. About how I have to *choose* to do a thing, but whenever I *do* choose, it ends up being different from what everybody wants me to do, and the rules get changed. And everybody knows more than me. I'm sick of it, Grey Bones."

His lips twitched in a smile more natural than the last. "I can only tell you what I have been told."

She spread her hands. "Apologies. Please continue."

"I must report on your condition as soon as you wake up. Assist you as you get ready, and then deliver you to the front door where a car is waiting."

"Who's in the car?"

He looked down at the floor. "Tiber Caruso."

She snorted a bitter chuckle. "Figures. Satan couldn't leave it to chance, could he?"

His face paled. "Don't …"

"Don't what? What happens if I decide not to go?"

"You will be taken."

"I was four feet away, and you jumped back like you saw a mouse go for your balls. To be taken, I need to be touched, right?"

"Oh, I won't touch you."

"Then who will?"

The door opened, and Carl walked in with his head down. She pushed off from the window before the door closed behind him. Into his arms and crying into his chest. The same old song and dance.

He stroked her hair. Rubbed his hand down her back.

She pushed away and looked up into his face. Whole and healed. Back to the craggy relief of a life lived too hard. To her, it was perfect. "I thought you were dead."

"I was."

She remembered holding his hand. Had the spark

brought him back? She didn't want an answer. She just wanted *him*.

"I don't know what to do," he whispered.

She put her forehead against his chest. "You're alive."

"For now."

She didn't need to ask what that meant. She looked up. Rose onto her toes. It felt like the first kiss. The last one.

The *only* one.

"I'm sorry," he said into her lips.

She shook her head. Silenced him with another kiss. Pulled him into a fierce hug. Her nightmare was leading her somewhere. Might as well find out.

She turned back to Greyson. "Can I get some clothes?"

He nodded. "There is already a selection in the closet behind you. When you are ready, just step into the hall. Mr. Iglesias will direct you through the facility."

"I'm gonna take my time."

He shrugged as he passed. "It won't matter."

Carl chuckled. "The story of my life."

The door clicked shut, and they stood alone. She knew they couldn't remain like that forever, but she knew her grip would lose strength eventually.

She turned away from him. Trailed her fingers down his arm.

The closet was full of clothes that could have come from her own drawers. Casual yet fashionable. As if a thing like looking good mattered at a time like this. The bathroom had a small shower. All the tools of beauty arranged on the vanity.

Carl stood in the open door and watched her. The lines in his face deepened with each passing minute. The corners of his mouth drew down. The joy left his body. Each small touch and embrace was more desperate than the last.

When she was ready, she opened the door without a word. Stepped into the silent hallway. Deep carpet and more wood paneling and trim. Plastered ceilings and ornate switch plate covers.

She saw not a single person on their way to the elevators. Heard no voices. Only the creaking of an old building settling in the sun. The hum of the motors. The bell when they reached the ground floor.

The doors opened onto a lobby as opulent as the Viazo Grand's. No front desk. Just doors marked with brass signs. Polished granite floors.

Mirrors on either side sent their reflections into infinity.

A wall of glass on the front of the building. A single step down into the lane under a wide awning. A long silver car sat waiting.

Carl pointed at it. "They said I can't go with you."

She took Carl's hand as they walked to the front door. She didn't want to say anything. The silent threat from Greyson in her room. The vision of those defenseless children at the clinic.

What was there to talk about?

She decided there was just one thing. Before opening the door, she stopped. Turned into him and looked up into his crying eyes. "I love you."

He nodded. "I love you too." His words were a gasp of air. Hissed emotion.

She put her hand flat on his chest. "I didn't even know what it felt like to love someone until I met you."

He nodded in agreement. Pressed his lips together. She smiled. "I wish so much for you. Not for *me*. For you. To be happy."

His face collapsed into sorrow. He had been holding it back from her, but she could tell it was too much. She held onto her smile. "This dream fucking sucks," she said.

He pulled her against him. His body shook as he sobbed. The vibration felt like waves slapping against the side of her boat.

She forced herself out of his arms. Stepped back. "When I wake up, I hope you're there."

Before he could respond, she spun around and marched outside. As her feet hit the concrete step outside, the back door of the silver car swung open.

Cream-colored leather seats. The sparkle of crystal glasses. Burled walnut bar lined with bottles full of various liquor.

She ducked inside, and the door closed by itself. She kept her eyes down, ignoring the man in the seat next to her. The car was so wide, it felt like she wouldn't be able to touch him even if she forced a stretch.

The car pulled forward without any engine noise. Just the crunch of the wheels as they rotated. They emerged from under the awning, and the windows darkened.

"That's a neat trick," she said.

A hoarse chuckle from the side. "I quite like it, yes."

She looked over, but she already knew what she would see. The face of the man on the shore. The smile that hung over her in the Viazo Grand. The man that was haunting her dreams inside her dream.

"Is it magic?" she asked.

He tipped his head. "No, just a technology so advanced as to appear so."

"Gotcha."

He was dressed in gray trousers. A red sweater over a white shirt. His tie matched his pants. His black cane was planted between his feet, and his shaking hands rested on the handle. It looked like a silver gargoyle. "Do you know my name?"

"Like in the Rolling Stones song?"

He shook his head, but his smile widened. "I'll not ask for sympathy, no. My name is Tiber Caruso."

She held her hand out as a joke. "Mickayla Waters. Pleased to meet you."

Before she could lower her hand, he reached out and took it in a firm grasp. Pumped it twice before letting it go. "The pleasure is mine."

He tipped his head back and laughed at the shock on her face. "I'm sorry. I thought you knew. For me, you have to *choose* to release the spark."

"Why?"

"Because I am not a child who has been scarred by kerosene flames. A *touch* of the spark is not for a being such as I. No, miss Waters, I need the whole thing."

She nodded. "That makes sense."

"Has anyone told you *anything*?"

She shrugged. "I figure I won't know something until I make it up. Like, the dream will actually change to cover it up, or I'll figure things out for myself."

"So, you think you're dreaming? Perhaps dying?"

She pointed a finger gun at him. Like Kristophel at her kitchen table. "Bingo."

One of his eyebrows lifted in consideration. "That will make negotiations more difficult."

She spread her hands. "How can I believe any of this is real? Like my whole life, I keep coming out on top ... so to speak."

He leaned forward and looked into her eyes. She cursed her tendency to like older men. He really was hand-some and charming. "How so?" he asked. Even his voice ... smooth and seductive. Deep and powerful, but with a kind charm. He smiled as he waited for her to answer.

She looked away from his gaze. There was a shadow

on the other side of the glass that separated the driver from the passenger. She could just make out his little hat.

"Oh, you know," she said. "Just an extension of how I've been lucky my whole life."

"It doesn't seem very lucky to me."

"That's what I thought, but here I am. Still kicking. So, why don't we cut to the chase?"

He leaned back, and his face became thoughtful. "Very well. It is, after all, bare simplicity. Take my hand. Willingly and completely. Pass the spark. Heal me, so I can be reborn in balance."

"To oppose Heaven, right? The whispering voice of temptation to all mankind?"

His brows drew down. "I'm afraid that is a bit inaccurate. As hard as it is to believe, I serve the Lord as do most."

"Right. Like his divine plan makes you."

He lifted one shoulder and ducked his head. "If you will. Which is a word most don't consider."

"What? *Will?*"

He nodded. "Yes." His eyes brightened as he leaned forward with excitement. "You see. As all mortals, *you* have a will, whereas I do not."

"So then how do you decide anything?"

"But I don't. It is decided *for* me."

"That doesn't make any sense."

"Child, you just don't understand. For you, time is chronological. It is entropy. It is the fulfillment of His gift to you. I see time as a moment that exists in an instant while stretching to infinity. I seem to you to *do* things. To attempt to alter things, but that is simply incorrect. I watch the moments unfold in human understanding. Enlightened by the choices you make."

She growled in frustration. "But doesn't that change what you do next?"

"No, for it has already been decided."

She drove her fist into her thigh. "That is just dumb and confusing."

He waved her protest aside. Leaned back into the cushion. "If every human could understand, then all would be gods."

She copied him. Nestled back into her seat with a sigh. "I'm not going to do it."

"So it would seem."

"You going to try to convince me?"

"I already have."

She rolled her eyes. "That's right. *Your* choices have already been made for you. Like some retroactive forgiveness. Some bullshit excuse where you don't have to take responsibility for your sins."

"Do you really wish to know?"

"Absolutely."

"Then we will discover it together."

"What does that mean?"

He lifted a shaking hand to point out her window. She realized the car was no longer moving. The windows brightened to reveal the front of the Sanctum Glorianis. She whistled in appreciation. "Now that was a neat trick."

He grinned. "That one *was* magic."

She sat back and laughed. Crossed her arms across her stomach. The car rocked as he opened his door and stepped out with a grunt of effort.

She caught her breath and wiped her eyes. She actually agreed with him. She couldn't wait to discover what was next. When the spark stayed silent inside her, she clamped down on her laughter.

She swallowed, but the sudden dread didn't subside.

Her door opened, and she looked up as Tiber Caruso stepped back and swept his hand aside. "If you please," he said.

She climbed out, and as she stood up, he took her arm. She wasn't sure which of them was offering support.

He smelled like leather and wood char. His skin was like dry sand. Her hand was in his, and his other hand fell to pat her wrist.

"Once we enter that door, you will see what I have to offer."

She leaned into him like he was a favorite uncle. He drew away in surprise, but after a moment, he settled. "You are remarkable. It is a shame what needs to be done to you."

Her dread grew into fear. A nervous excitement that twisted in her gut. "I forgive you."

It felt right to say.

He staggered, and his cane slipped from his grasp. It clattered against the bottom step. He panted like he had run laps through the courtyard. "You don't know the value of your words."

She shrugged as she bent to retrieve the cane. The silver handle felt cold and slick. Like the slime on top of rotting meat. She passed it back. Held him up while he regained his composure.

He took a deep breath and squared his shoulders. "Shall we?"

She nodded, and they took the first step together. It felt like she was walking deeper into her nightmare. Maybe into Hell itself. She remembered climbing the stairs with Kristophel. "Let's," she said.

At least she was in good company.

Chapter Seventeen

THE TRIP to the top of the steps was much shorter than she remembered it from last time. That fever dream Alice in Wonderland bullshit. She looked back over her shoulder as she reached the top, and the silver car was gone.

She hadn't heard it pull away.

She shrugged as she faced front. Instead of the door opening as before, with Lobster Marm stepping out in character, Mickayla stepped to the side while Tiber Caruso opened the door and ducked his head in invitation.

She nodded in thanks and walked across the threshold. The hallway was bright, but it extended well into the distance. A pinpoint of darkness at the end where the stairway led to the sunken gallery.

That was more like it.

She smiled as the old man closed the door and resumed his place by her side. He didn't take her hand this time. She looked down in confusion. Wondered why he would no longer touch her.

"We shall begin shortly," he said.

She nodded. "Okay." Water flowed out from under the doors on either side. A ripple that swept across the floor.

"You have been told you sacrificed for your sister," he said. She looked up at him. His lips were cracked and his teeth were flecked with blood. His shoulder stooped as if under a heavy weight. "But no," he continued. "It was *she* that made the sacrifice."

She waved him away. "You weren't there. You don't know what happened."

He pointed a palsied finger at the nearest door. "Perhaps not, but she was."

The door opened, and more water rushed out to join the gentle waves an inch deep across the floor. A little girl stood holding the doorknob. Blonde hair. Face chapped by the wind off the lake up in Winstead.

Rose looked exactly like she had the day she died. She waved. Her grin sunk her cheeks into twin dimples. "Hi, Mickey."

Mickayla waved back.

The door across the hall opened. More water poured into the hallway. It crested her toes. Soaked into her laces.

The little girl in the other door was blue and wrinkled. Her eyes were covered in a silvery film. Like fish scales. Hair matted to her head hung down to cling to her cheeks and jaw. Her dimples were holes that revealed her rotten teeth. She waved, and her skin split at the elbow to show white bone beneath. "Hi, Mickey."

Mickayla waved back.

Tiber Caruso planted his cane and took a grunting step. Mickayla followed along. Splashed through the rising water. It licked at her ankles. Her toes were numb lumps of lead.

He pointed ahead with his cane before planting it for another step. "It is the soul that is important. For it offers no protection against me. You, on the other hand … you are a blind spot. Only my mortal eyes can see you, but the threads of time knit over your existence as if you were a whiff of smoke."

He brought the tips of his fingertips to his mouth. Blew on them and opened his hand like he was releasing a captured moth.

The next door opened. Instead of a curious child with a lantern, it was another Rose. Older than the first. Hair in two ponytails. A stuffed lamb held to her chest. "Hi, Mickey."

Mickayla waved.

Another dead Rose opened the opposite door for her own greeting, but Mickayla lowered her head. Studied the swirling water that was now above the middle of her shin.

"What do you want?" she whispered.

"Why, I want you to understand."

She glanced over, and his eyes were weeping black oil into his crow's feet. Crusting the corners of his lips to mix with the fresh blood seeping from his gums.

"You see. I have her now. Thanks to your friend Kristophel, I have her *forever*. To burn and torture and *hurt* as I will."

Another door, and another Rose stepped out. Eleven or twelve years old. Mickayla remembered what it had been like. The confusion of early puberty. Already filling out. Wilting under the gaze of men that should have known better.

Rose took her hand off the doorknob to plant it on her hip. Her knowing smile deepened those dimples, and Mickayla wanted to tell the little girl to put a bra on.

Rose waved. "Hey, Mickey."

The opposite door opened, and a rotting Rose stepped out to join her healthy doppelganger. "Hey."

Her voice was a hollow hiss.

Water carried strings of dark blood into the hallway. Cold waves against her knees. She leaned into the force of the water. Tiber Caruso put more of his weight on the cane as he struggled to continue.

"And then there's your friends," he said. His eyes were glistening pools of black. His nails were cracking points of bone protruding from the ends of his fingers.

"What friends?" she asked.

"Come now. We all have them. He put his hand on his chest. "Even I have friends."

The fourth door opened, and Rose leaned against the jam. Wearing the bathing suit Mickayla wore a week before she jumped into Johnny Denton's pool. The day she fucked him in his basement rec room.

"Hey, Mick," Rose said.

Mickayla looked at the end of the hall when the other door opened. The water that rushed out carried a surge of dirty black tendrils full of squirming bugs.

The water was mid-thigh. Bitter cold. The bugs clung to her jeans. Crawled in slow circles like they were blind. She was afraid to brush them off. Having them on her skin would make her scream.

The water was almost to her crotch.

"It is simple," Tiber Caruso said. "I will have them. Your friends. The demon at the hotel where you pleasure the old men. The angel who fancies himself a victim."

Mickayla lifted her hands in a shrug. "I mean, Amanda, sure. I've always thought of her as a friend. The demon thing is new. Just something I made up for this dream, but yeah, she's a friend. Calling Kristoballs my friend is a stretch."

Another door opened. Rose stepped out in a form-fitting dress. A cigarette hanging between her fingers. The key to the back door of the Viazo Grand dangled from a chain around her wrist.

Her hair and makeup were perfect. Mickayla never remembered looking so amazing, but they *were* twins. "Hey, kid," Rose said.

Tiber Caruso ducked his head as the door across the hall opened. "Perhaps *friend* was incorrect, but there is still Mr. Iglesias."

The Rose from the other door was mostly skeleton. Rotten flesh clinging to bones with bleeding threads of tissue. She waved with a hand mostly gone to decay. She had no lips to form words, but her voice issued through her teeth like a dry wind.

The water crept above her waistband.

"And the children," Tiber Caruso said.

A building current at her back kept her from stomping to a halt. "What children?" she demanded.

He spread his hands. His neck had lengthened. His head hung like it had grown beyond his body's ability to hold it up. "Any children. *All* children. You can make of it what you will."

She saw them collected at her feet. Looking up at her in joyous gratitude. She shook her head to deny the memory. She didn't deserve thanks and praise.

Another door opened. Rose held herself against the rush of water at her back. Clung to the door frame with scarecrow fingers.

She was gaunt. Pale and hollow. Dark circles under her eyes. Thin skin stretched over protruding bones, and Mickayla brought her hands to her mouth. Rose caught her balance. Put a cigarette in her mouth. Clinked open the Zippo to light it.

"I'll see you later, kid," she said through a cloud of smoke.

The other door didn't open.

"I don't know what you're trying to tell me," Mickayla whined.

Tiber Caruso pushed through water that had risen to his chest. It was almost up to her armpits, and her toes kept lifting from the floor. The bugs had penetrated the denim, and she felt burning bites as they tried to burrow into her skin. She couldn't bring herself to reach under the water to wipe them away.

She looked to the end of the hall, and the opening to the stairs was closer than she expected. It had looked a mile away when they started walking. Now it was within a few steps. A final pair of doors on either side before they would get there.

The door on the right opened, and the water carried the lifeless body of her dead sister into the hallway. Mickayla reached out to grab the body as it floated away. Toward the top of the stairs, and the sound of the water became a roar.

Spray hit her in the face. She reached out for support, and Tiber Caruso caught her hand in his. He pulled her close and his mouth was full of a jumble of sharp bone. She pulled back in a panic, and the roar of the water intensified. "It means," he hissed in her ear, "I will remove your choice with a promise."

His breath smelled like rotten fish. Entrails baking in the sun. Infection and corruption. "Everything you hold dear — even as an *idea* of love inside your pathetic diseased consciousness — I will ruin. For as long as I hold dominion in Hell, I will make every person you have *ever* touched ... suffer."

The force of the water at her back pushed her over the edge. As she tipped over the top step, she looked back at the final door. It burst open under the pressure, and instead of water, a wash of blackness came out.

The thunder of crashing water. The howling of distant hounds. Dark laughter underneath her own screams, and she went under. Her face scraped along the carpeted stairs as the current pushed her down. The water filled with the billowing ink of Tiber Caruso's evil, and she was surrounded by the slick oil that had supported her when this nightmare first began in Room Number Three.

It filled her mouth. Burned into her nose. She clamped her lips together. Closed her eyes. tumbled along like a rudderless ship in a tidal wave.

She felt little fingers in hers. The terrified grip of her drowning sister. Before she could pull her twin to her chest to wrap her in the protection of her arms, her head crashed into the floor, and her hand sprung open.

Her vision flooded with light as she popped above the surface of the black flood. The plummeting water rushed her toward the wooden railing at the top of the gallery. The dark water crashed over the edge, and she was swept along with it.

She screamed as she felt the weight leave her in her descent, and her voice cut off with the impact. Flat on her back on the edge of the stage. The thick water beat against her like a hundred switches swiping against her exposed body.

She took a gagging breath. Felt the dark bugs in her mouth. Wriggling in her hair. The echo of her fresh scream came back to her, and she opened her eyes to look at the floor between her hands. Her guts heaved, and she vomited a stream of black oil onto her splayed fingers.

She caught her breath as the sound of the raging river fell to a distant roar. Then there was nothing but a constant drip. A counterpoint to her wet panting.

She sat back on her heels. On the stage in front of her was a quivering mass of shining blackness. Like a roiling pile of melted plastic. A skin of black blood coated its surface.

The mass expanded. Two large flaps of material lifted away. Wings. Tipped in wicked points. Connected to a dark body that rose as powerful legs gathered beneath it. A white segmented stripe of flesh ran down the center of the creature's belly. Translucent flesh that showed the churning insides.

The beast stood to its full height. A head that looked like the coals of a raging fire rippled with heat. Two eyes as hollow as distant space. Black and spinning with dark power. Its mouth opened, and it ducked to howl into her face.

Heat that tightened her skin and blew her wet hair from her forehead. A choking smoke that burned her eyes.

Its wings spread to their limits, filling her view with nothing but oil-slicked leather. Roping muscles. Cracked skin with lava flowing in smoking channels. The beast stepped back to press its back against the wall. Lifted its trailing leg to tuck under its body as it sat, and three tables were revealed on the stage. Each covered in a fluttering white sheet.

She stood up. Swayed on her feet as she fought for balance. She waved her hand in a line that included all three tables. "Is this it?"

The beast panted a smoking breath into the floor. Rivulets of dripping oil spread in seeking tendrils from its clawed feet.

IT IS

The voice was the sound of despair. Pain echoing through every scream that had ever been heard. She cried out and covered her ears, but she couldn't block the sound of it cutting into her heart.

YOU WILL CHOOSE FOR I GROW WEARY

She dropped her hands. Looked up at it through the fall of her wet hair. She pointed at the table on her right. "The fuck is under that?"

The beast settled in to watch, and light swirled in its eyes.

BEHOLD

The sheet fell away.

Chapter Eighteen

"WHAT ARE YOU GONNA DO, KID?" Rose said.

Mickayla shouted in wordless joy. The emptiness that Rose had left behind when she disappeared was filled again, and Mickayla dropped back to her knees to bend forward as her sobs doubled her over.

"I never left. He took me. You let go just like last time."

Mickayla sat up straight. "What?"

Rose didn't answer. But the silence felt intentional. Like she had chosen to be quiet instead of being … gone.

Mickayla wiped at her tears. The slick of black on her skin burned her eyes. She pushed herself to her feet. Turned to the first table.

"There you go, kid," Rose said. "You asked for it."

Blood flowed in slow drips from the edge of the table. A hand flopped over the edge. All the fingers were missing except for the first one. It was encircled by a silver ring.

"Don't look at me, darling," Amanda gasped.

Half of her face was charred and black. The eye looking out of the damage was full of blood. Wide and staring without the protection of an eyelid. The skin along her jaw had crisped and split, and Mickayla could see her tongue moving between her teeth as she swallowed.

Mickayla took a small step. Held her hands out in front of her. Like trying to calm an angry dog.

Amanda turned her face away. Humped and rocked on the table to move to the far edge, but she was limited by the filthy restraints that held her down. "You musn't," she shouted. "Just let me be."

The spark welled up inside her. It rode the wave of her sympathy and guilt, and her hands stretched forward.

"Didn't you hear what she said?" Rose asked.

Mickayla nodded. Dropped her hands. Looked down at the floor.

"Let her go," Rose said. "It's what you do best."

Mickayla hugged herself. Dug her fingers into the fabric of her dripping shirt. Forced herself to look up at Amanda's tortured body.

The destruction was random. From superficial to deep. Burns and slashes. Smear of blood and gore across pale skin. She looked like an abstract painter's representation of a woman.

Amanda strained against her bonds. Stretched her neck up and rolled her eyes to look at the beast resting in the corner. "I have accepted what he has done to me. So must you."

Mickayla shook her head. "He's killing you."

"Darling, no. He is welcoming me home."

"I don't understand."

She heard the storm echo off the water. The shouts of her parents. Rose's cry for help in the distance.

"You gonna listen to it this time, Mickey?" Rose asked.

Mickayla's hand trembled as it came around from her side. She told herself it was the spark. Closed her eyes as she reached to end Amanda's suffering.

"You dumb fucking cunt!"

Mickayla jumped back from the venom she heard in Amanda's voice. Pulled her hand back in flutter under her chin.

Amanda's eyes matched her anger. One forced open by injury. The other one wide with emotion. "You cannot do this. He is tempting you. He is testing you. He is …"

Her eyes relaxed. Stuttered closed. She settled back on the table.

Mickayla took another small step, but she kept her hands close. "I still don't understand."

"You need to take responsibility," Rose said.

Mickayla looked up at the ceiling. "Responsibility for what?"

Rose's pleas for rescue were louder now. Closer.

Mickayla looked back at Amanda. Her friend licked her lips. "She is telling you to take responsibility for what you have caused."

Instead of responding to what Amanda said, she put her hands on her hips. "You can hear her now?"

Rose's sigh blew past her ear. "She's *always* been able to hear me."

"I could always hear her," Amanda confirmed.

Mickayla turned so the monster was at her back. She could feel the heat of his gaze burning across her shoulders. "I don't know what to do."

"Stop avoiding," Rose said.

Mickayla spread her hands. "I'm trying to heal her. To make her better."

"She doesn't want it, kid."

"I need to pay her back."

"For what?"

Mickayla closed her eyes. Looked back on her first time in Amanda's office. She had liked her in an instant.

"And why was that?" Rose asked.

Mickayla shrugged. "She was nice."

"Bullshit."

Tears squeezed between her clenched eyelids. "She took me in."

"She fucking *used* you."

"She was my friend."

"Doesn't change the facts, kid."

Amanda sat behind her desk like a queen. Tipped her head back and looked at Mickayla with uncertainty. "How many men have you fucked?"

Mickayla shrugged.

Amanda lifted one eyebrow. "More than twenty?"

Mickayla nodded. "Definitely."

"More than thirty?"

Mickayla shrugged. "Probably."

"Are you clean?"

Dr. Bailey always said so, often with a tone of disbelief. "Yes," Mickayla said.

Amanda smiled. "Do you do drugs?"

Mickayla nodded without hesitation. "Yes."

Amanda's smile became a grin. Her teeth were small and even. Perfectly aligned and sparkling white.

"This may be your lucky day, then."

Mickayla relaxed at the other woman's change in attitude. "Why is that?" she asked.

Amanda steepled her fingers. "The men to whom we cater are not the sick fuckers you may be used to, if I may presume."

Mickayla tipped her head in acknowledgment. Many of her recent relationships had not been on the healthy side, but there had always been something about them that had satisfied some need. Some deep desire.

"This job," Amanda continued, "is difficult by some

standards. Easy by others. Older gentlemen who will pay for a young woman of uncommon appearance. Carl said, and I quote, this chick is fucking insane, bro. I believe him as I usually do, but he was wrong only in a matter of degree. Room Number Three is open, and I will take you there now."

She stood and stretched. Like a panther getting ready to pace along with the herd, and Mickayla felt like prey under the older woman's sudden intense scrutiny.

It was exciting.

Amanda held her hand out. "Let's see what you're up for."

When it was over, Rose wondered why they had never slept with a woman before. In fact, she was *surprised* that it had never happened. Mickayla agreed with a satisfied smile and a cigarette. It turned out she had been up for quite a bit.

"Your *friend* is a fucking predator, kid."

Mickayla felt the chill of the water. Felt the choking pressure as it closed over her head. Her hand was tight inside her sister's tiny grip.

Rose whispered in her ear. "What do you really want?"

Mickayla pressed her fists into her belly. "I don't know."

"Bullshit."

"I want to …"

"What?" Rose said.

They both sank under the surface.

"I just want …"

"Spit it out for fuck's sake."

"To be forgiven," Mickayla whispered.

Her lungs burned. Her heart hammered in her chest. The darkness became complete. The noise of the water filled her ears with confusion and panic. Her fingers loosened.

"Really?" Rose said. "Is that *really* what you want?"

Her sister's weight was too much. She was afraid of never seeing the surface again. Never hearing her mother's voice. Never playing with her toys.

"No," Mickayla said.

Amanda's breath sounded like trickling water. "Tell her what you want, darling. I saw it when I first met you. I see it now."

Her sister's little hand was forced. The grip was painful. They were being pulled deeper and deeper. Farther from shore.

"It was your fault," Mickayla said.

"Was it?" Rose responded.

"You rocked the boat. You wouldn't sit down."

Amanda snorted laughter. Choked and coughed. Gasped for a deep breath. "She would never have hurt you. *Never*."

She felt Rose's nod. "Can you say the same?"

Mickayla shook her head. "No."

The beast rumbled with pleasure. A deep vibration that emanated from the floorboards.

"You told me to stop," Mickayla said. "I was just having fun. But you were so scared …"

Her feet were planted up against either side. She was almost in the splits. Rose laughed at her, and Mickayla started shuffling her feet closer to get her stance back to normal, but the boat began to wiggle.

Mickayla threw her head back and laughed. Pushed into the wiggle, and Rose started laughing too.

"But I wasn't," Rose said.

Mickayla turned to face the creature looming over the stage, but she kept her eyes closed. "No, you weren't laughing," Mickayla said. "You were crying. Begging for me to stop. You were so fucking scared, and I just kept laughing."

The shock of falling in made her gasp in a lungful of water. Coughing and gagging until it felt like somebody was pulling her insides out right through her ribs. Rose clung to her shoulders. Scratched bloody furrows into the back of her neck in her panic.

"Why were we even out there?" Mickayla said.

She felt Rose's shrug. "They said the storm was coming. Told us no. Neither one of us liked being told *no*."

Mickayla thought she was going to die. Rose held on as tightly as she could. Desperate for her sister to save her. But Mickayla wanted to live. Instinct or spite?

She didn't know. She opened her fingers. Pushed Rose away with her other hand. Kicked to the surface. Right into the waiting arms of her rescuers.

"They were right there," she said. "One more second, and they would have gotten us both."

"But you let me go," Rose said. "Then you pushed me away."

Mickayla nodded.

"Then tell us what you really want."

Mickayla opened her eyes. Looked up into the burning eyes of the monster. "I want to suffer."

She turned and walked to the foot of Amanda's table. "Why do I love you?"

Amanda stared straight ahead. A fixed point on the ceiling. "Why do you love *anybody*?"

The beast stood. Its shadow grew to cover Amanda's head. Tendrils of crawling oil crept closer. Its breath washed across them like the wind from a carrion-filled desert.

Mickayla set her hands on the blood-caked wood.

Looked at the broken and torn toes. Protruding bones. Exposed fat. "When will I wake up?"

"When you answer me," Amanda gasped.

Mickayla nodded. "I love you because I *choose* to."

"Then let me go."

Mickayla stepped back. Her hand was cold. Suddenly devoid of the heat from Rose's grip. She scrubbed her palm on her jeans. Felt the oily bodies of the bugs burst under the pressure. "I let my sister go," she said.

"I know," Amanda whispered.

"I pushed her away."

"I know."

"I hate myself so fucking much."

The beast towered above them, but she refused to look at it. It was no worse than her, and she had looked at herself every day for her whole life. She already knew what a monster looked like.

Amanda convulsed. Choked on her indrawn breath. The beast leaned over her and tilted its head down to hang over Amanda's face.

REDEMPTION

The voice slid into her mind like the shining skin that held intestines together.

MY CHILD COME BACK TO ME

Amanda's final sigh sounded like somebody thrust their fist into a bowl of pudding. The tension left her neck and abdomen. One eye closed. The other rolled up.

The beast swept one wing over her body, and the wind of its passage boiled the flesh from the bones. Bubbled the fluids into black stains. Rendered the remains to ash.

Two crashing steps put the monster in its resting position at the back of the stage. It hunkered down with a sigh that sounded like a jet of flame from a blast furnace.

"Why did you let me go?" Rose said.

Mickayla shrugged.

"Why did you push me away?"

Mickayla shook her head. She couldn't even explain it to herself. Only the guilt was real.

"Why did you give me your soul?"

"I wanted you to live?"

'That's not true. If you had wanted me to live, you would have saved me."

"I didn't want to die."

"Join the fucking club."

"I was so scared."

"Come on. You did it for the same reason those career sinners repent on their deathbeds. A little forgiveness makes everything okay."

Mickayla pushed her clinging hair back from her face. "I don't deserve forgiveness."

"Amanda was right. You *are* dumb. Don't you get it? You *already* have my forgiveness. That's not something you earn. It's something you have because I fucking love you. So much it hurts deep inside. I *understand*. And I *love* you. And I *forgive* you."

Mickayla could no longer hold her head up. Her hands dropped next to her thighs. Her knees shook with the effort to stay on her feet.

Rose forgave her. She could barely comprehend it. And the fact that the forgiveness had always been there. Even further beyond understanding.

"Oh, Mickey," Rose said. "The point is not to have somebody else forgive you. It's for you to forgive yourself."

The sheet on the second table fluttered as if the body underneath exhaled a long sigh.

The beast laughed with the sound of cracking ice.

BEHOLD

The second sheet fell away.

Chapter Nineteen

It was a large man with dark skin. Burned and torn as Amanda had been. his black hair spilled over the side, and Mickayla cried out as she rushed to the head of the table. "No no no no …"

She skidded in the spread of slick blood on the floor. Her thighs crashed into the table with the sound of splitting wood. She pressed her hands to either side of the man's face. Gasped in fresh recognition. Then again when she felt the guilt.

She had thought the man was Carl. In spite of what he had said back at the sanitorium, she saw him there. Broad chest and shoulders. Dark features. But it was Kristophel instead.

She couldn't help her sweeping relief. The shame that followed it.

His eyes fluttered open, but there was nothing but bloody gel behind his eyelids. Black blood oozed from the corners to trickle down his temples and into his matted hair.

"Ah," he said. "There you are."

She smiled and nodded. "Here I am."

He lifted his hand, but it only came off the table a couple of inches before snapping against the soaked canvas strap.

He growled in frustration, and Mickayla snatched her hand back to cover her mouth. His stomach had been slit open, and when he breathed, the edges separated to reveal the glistening viscera of his intestines.

She bit back the spasm in her throat. Swallowed the acid and lowered her hand back to his face.

She shushed him. Stroked his cheek. "Don't talk. Just … I don't know what to do."

"Are you trying to heal him?" Rose asked.

Mickayla rocked back and forth in frustration. "I don't know. It's not working."

"Why should it?"

"Because I fucking want it to," Mickayla said.

Kristophel grinned. His teeth were broken. Many were missing. The dark blood sparkled as he tipped his head to direct his voice toward where she stood above him. "Why do you want to heal me, child?"

She closed her eyes. "Because."

"Come closer," he said.

She opened her eyes and bent down. Her tears dripped onto his cheeks.

"Why do you cry for me?"

"I don't know."

"Or do you cry for another?"

"I don't *know*."

His throat sounded like a peppercorn grinder when he swallowed, and his mouth twisted with a grimace of pain. "Cry for yourself child, for I am bound for glory."

She was in a cave. She sat next to a flickering torch. Kristophel sat on the rocky floor next to her. Blood splattered his polished armor. Dried in the creases of his knuckles. Streaked his face and hair. He turned to her, and his dark eyes were full of despair.

His shoulders shook with his sobs.

"Why does He ask it of me?" he said, and his voice cracked with emotion.

Her heart filled with sympathy for the angel. She knew the sacrifice he made for his obedience. She reached out and put her hand on his shoulder pauldron. The bronze segment of armor was as warm as skin.

Kristophel sagged in relief. Leaned his head over to rest his cheek on her knuckles.

She took a calming breath and closed her eyes. "If I could but heal you, bold Kristophel."

"Lord, how I suffer."

She opened her eyes to meet the angel's gaze. His lips peeled back from his teeth, and he shook his head. "I rape and murder. Steal and lie. All for His mercy. At His whim. And I sin further by questioning Him. I deserve damnation."

She shook her head. "No, Kristophel. You deserve salvation, for you have been poorly used."

"Lord, I suffer," Kristophel whispered.

Wind blew in from the cave opening, and the torch went out with a hiss. The swirl of black smoke was revealed in the light that grew in the angel's chest.

He lifted his cheek from her hand. Squared his shoulders. "But I obey," he said.

She pulled her hand back. "It is always hard in the dim of the night. But when the sin renews, so shall you. Revel in His light, good Kristophel. Your reward is long nigh, and well-deserved, but there is terrible work yet to do."

Scraping footsteps from outside, and a cohort of angels ducked inside. They saluted her with downcast eyes as they gathered at Kristophel's back. Lesser beings than the great winged creation so full of sorrow, yet still full of powerful beauty as to represent the Will of the Lord.

They placed their hands on his shoulders. His back. His head. Kristophel closed his eyes and accepted their grace. If required by God, he would betray them, but for now, they were brothers and sisters united in light and purpose.

"To battle," Kristophel said.

They left her in the dark, and she bowed her head in shame.

She opened her eyes to look into his empty gaze. "You see now?"

She shook her head. "I don't know why that keeps happening."

"The *why* is not important."

"But what does it mean?"

His hideous grin closed, and his face became thoughtful. "And that is not a why."

She felt Rose press into her like she was trying to see over her shoulder. "*What* did you see, not *why* did you see it."

"This is not my punishment," Kristophel said. "This is my reward."

"The spark," Rose whispered.

She heard the beast become unsettled behind her. A rustling like giant scales sliding over each other as a serpent slithered into knots. Its hiss brought boiling heat across her back.

Kristophel gasped in pain.

Mickayla shook her head. "It won't heal him."

"No, dummy. It *can't* heal him. That's what was in the vision."

Kristophel moaned. Pushed his head into her right hand, like he was trying to nuzzle her palm. "I have fulfilled thousands of years of purpose, child. Finally, I have committed my final sin. It was against you, and I beg nothing more of you."

She closed her eyes, and she saw the smiling boy in the desert. Walking without his crutches on straight and strong legs.

Peter's hands as he spread water over her feet.

The villagers looking up at her from the river.

Kristophel's pain from the cave.

The pure joy of reaching out to transfer the divine power of the spark into a damaged soul.

She gasped in understanding. Christ's power was reflected in his touch. An echo of it had been saved in the scrap of hem from the robes he wore while performing miracles.

She was living the last remnants of a life that had once saved the world.

Kristophel sighed. "You see."

She shook her head. "No."

Rose was next to her ear. "Healing him would make you feel better, but keeping him here would deny him his reward."

Kristophel nodded. "She is right, child. Stop punishing yourself, for there is always another that suffers with you."

Mickayla dropped her hands. Stepped back. She walked around to stand at the foot of the table. Found a clean spot on the floor to place her feet. She didn't want to stand in his blood.

"Are you still there?" he asked.

"No," she said.

His laughter surprised her, but it soon fell into liquid coughing. He sighed, then lay still. She wondered if this was finally where the nightmare ended.

"Not likely," Rose said.

A crash of thunder drove her heart against her ribs. She jumped with a squeal and looked up at the ceiling. A glowing dot formed in the center. Expanded into a roaring flame of gold.

The beast collapsed into a small tangle of limbs. Pulled its wings in to wrap around itself. Its growl sounded like the fading echoes of the light's appearance.

A beautiful song formed in her mind. A chorus. Joyous and worshipful. Clear trumpets. The spark swelled inside her, and she grinned at the building light above her.

Trackers emerged from the glow. Glorious wings spread to scrape along the walls as they descended.

BROTHER

Their cry was a long-awaited cheer for a returning son.

She recognized the smiling faces of the angels from her vision. Standing over Kristophel in fellowship. They settled to the stage to stand in a circle that included her in the center.

She wanted to duck and back away. Slip between them so their moment could be theirs alone.

NAY LITTLE SISTER WITNESS AND REJOICE

Kristophel's body was light. A flame that burned her image away. She could no longer see the torn and twisted form of his body broken on the table.

In its place was the beautiful form of the angel. The one she had first seen in Room Number Three. Exquisite and pure.

She clasped her hands together and watched him rise

from the stained wood. He held his hands out, and his smile was like morning sunshine.

They spread their wings as one, and they crashed them down with the power and thunder of their arrival. Force that shook the world, and they shot into the light still clinging to the ceiling.

She was left hollow with having seen such a thing. A sight that would never repeat. Could never hold in her mind. She fell to her knees. Held the edge of the table for support as she wept with joy.

Rose's hand was on her shoulder. "How about now?" she asked.

Mickayla caught her breath. Shook her head. "How about now *what*?"

Rose sighed. "Why is it so hard with you?"

Mickayla stood. Clutched the table for balance. She looked at the beast still hiding behind its wings. "How can I do it?" She pointed at the ceiling. "After seeing that shit, how can I *ever* do what you want?"

The black wings opened like spreading ink. The baleful stare of the monster hung above the smiling split of its burning mouth. It stood to fill the back of the stage with shadow.

YOU REQUIRE MORE

She flinched away from the force of its voice. "I don't require shit. I said *no*. I *deny* you!"

The spark felt like a burning coal in her chest. It bounced and fluttered like a blowtorch flame. Its hot approval made her flush. Sweat formed a slick between her shoulder blades. Trickled down her ribs.

"Dammit, Mickayla," Rose said. "You're a pain in the ass."

Mickayla lifted her finger to point at the beast's smiling face. "I deny you," she whispered.

"You're so dramatic," Rose said.

YOUR REQUIREMENT WILL BE HONORED

The beast was gone. In between one heartbeat and the next, it had ceased to exist.

Amanda's table was gone. So was Kristophel's.

A single table remained. White sheet draped over a still form. Blood dripped onto the floor in an undulating tempo.

"What is this?" Mickayla asked.

She smelled the water from Lake Winstead. Duckweed and fish.

The flowing tendrils of black oil on the floor stretched toward her like they were seeking her out by her scent. The pale white bodies of the squirming bugs floated to the surface. Dove back into the depths. Swam along the top. Wriggled and crawled along the wooden floor.

"Seriously," she said. She looked up. Spun in a circle, but there was nobody there. "What is this?"

The spark settled back into a dull warmth in her belly.

She threw her hands up in frustration. "Come on. What does any of this mean? What *do* I require?"

The only response was the splattering blood.

Mickayla waved at the empty gallery benches. "Hello?"

A breath behind her made her freeze. She closed her eyes. Shook her head in denial. "Rose?"

She thought her sister was gone again. But of course she wasn't.

Mickayla's throat burned. Why couldn't she just wake up?

"Are you still so sure of this nightmare?"

She spun around in surprise. Tiber Caruso stood at the edge of the stage. The cane directed to the floor between his feet. His hand covering the snarling head of the gargoyle handle. His pant legs were rolled up as if he was getting ready to splash in a puddle. Or wade out into a lake.

"What is this?" Mickayla demanded. "Where's Rose?"

He smiled. Concern and pity. He tipped his head. "She is where she has *always* been."

The third sheet fell away.

Chapter Twenty

ROSE WAS ON THE TABLE. Lips pressed together. She panted through her nose. Tears fell from her eyes to track clean stripes through the blood that caked her face.

Her skin was split in a bloody crisscross of slashes and cuts. Splintered ribs protruded to twitch in the air in time with her breath. Each joint bent at an unnatural angle. Her fingers and toes were twisted. Black with collected blood.

Mickayla screamed. Slipped in the tendrils of living oil as she jumped forward to run to the head of the table. She waved her hands for balance. Regained her footing. Made it to her sister to stand over her with her shoulders heaving as she begged her lungs for air.

She called on the spark floating inside her. The fire of its power. It rose up in response, and she put her hands on either side of Rose's face.

The power rushed out of her in a crescendo. Bones knit and skin closed. Joy filled Mickayla's heart at the sight of her sister becoming whole.

Rose screamed in agony. Piercing and desperate.

Mickayla jerked back in surprise, and the power of the spark rebounded into her. She rocked back on her feet. Slipped and dropped to one knee.

Rose was torn and bloody again, and her life poured off the edge of the table.

"NO!" Mickayla cried.

She pushed back to her feet and positioned herself back at her sister's head. Put her hands on either side of her face, and the spark jumped back in to release its healing power.

Rose's scream was loud and ragged. Her words were lost in the sheer breaking volume, but Mickayla heard the plea in her voice.

She pulled her hands away, and again the power slammed back into her. Rose was as she had been when the sheet first fell away. Terribly tortured and suffering, but her face was calm.

"Please," she said. "It hurts."

"I know," Mickayla said, and she stepped back up for another attempt.

Every time she touched her, Rose healed and screamed, and Mickayla had to let her go.

She couldn't count the number of times she tried.

Exhaustion seeped into her muscles. Her joints swelled. Bones ached. Her eyes burned. Still, Rose begged for the pain to stop.

"I'm trying, baby," Mickayla gasped.

"Are you?" Tiber Caruso was at her side, looking down at his handiwork. "Are you *really*?"

Mickayla hung her head. "Fuck you."

"She seems to be in quite a lot of pain."

"I know. What do you think I'm doing?"

"I think you are failing."

"Please," Rose whispered.

Mickayla lifted her hands to either side of her sister's face, and Rose took a deep gasping breath. "STOP!"

Mickayla stepped back. "I don't understand."

Tiber Caruso clucked his tongue. "It has been like this for your whole life. Stop hurting her."

Mickayla shook her head. Looked away from his kindly smile. "I'm not ... I'm trying to save her."

"Stop," Rose said. "Just stop it. Please ..."

Tiber Caruso gave a knowing sigh. "Yes, it would seem that *you* are the one hurting her."

She lowered her hands. They were covered in Rose's blood. Under her nails. In the lines of her palms.

Tiber Caruso's cane stumped on the floor as he maneuvered around the table to stand with his shoulder brushing hers. "It has ever been so," he said.

She looked up to see they were standing side by side on the edge of a cliff overlooking plains of sand. Tall grass and swaying palm trees in the distance.

"What say you now?" Tiber Caruso said.

She looked over at him. He was much as she remembered, only younger and darker. His cane was carved wood. The rough shape of the horned head under his hand.

She sighed, and turned back to the desert view. "As always, I deny your temptations."

Tiber Caruso chuckled. "They are not *my* temptations. They are merely what live in your own heart."

"So then I deny my heart."

"Then you deny humanity. The sickness in me grows even now. It is a matter of time."

"Part of my father's plan."

"So He would have us all believe."

She rolled a smooth pebble under her feet. Pushed it aside so it wouldn't dig into her knees when she later knelt to pray. "Why is it that you think He has not prepared for even this?"

Tiber Caruso shrugged. "I don't know. It's something I have struggled with. I see the beginning of the riddle. The middle. Even the *end*. Just not the solution."

"And you think He does not?"

"He has said as much. Tipped creation into motion. Down a predetermined path. So I must conclude it carries certain sureties."

She smiled at his arrogance. "Like your continued existence?"

Tiber Caruso lifted his cane. Drove the point into the ground for emphasis. "But what else is my purpose?"

She tipped her head. "It is not for you to know."

"So does that mean *you* know?"

She shook her head. "I am not trusted as much as you would believe. Like you, I am governed by my form. One that is not longed for this world. That is why you panic. Why you negotiate with temptation, but what you don't understand is I was not created merely to worship Him at His side. I do it out of *choice*. Out of love."

"I can offer you so much ..."

"You can offer me nothing that I have not already seen in His glorious light. *Nothing*."

Tiber Caruso hissed in frustration. "Then I do not understand what He wants of me."

She kicked another stone away from her. "Perhaps I can address your fears."

"With what?"

"I accept."

Tiber Caruso took a step to the side, and his cane fell from his hands. "You cannot mean what you say."

She held up one finger. "On behalf of another? I can."

Tiber Caruso held out a shaking hand. "Then touch

me, so your divinity will make me whole to continue His purpose in my existence."

She shook her head. "I think not."

The sun darkened to the color of blood. The wind warmed into blistering heat. Coals danced in the air. The crack of spreading wings was of the heavens splitting with thunder, but she didn't flinch.

She turned to face the great beast that Tiber Caruso had become. Smiled up into its burning face. "At the long end of the wheel's turn, you will have it, though the one that carries my spark may not know it. So the thing is up to you. My gift, Lucifer. Given in pity. Now begone, so that I may worship."

She turned to look at Tiber Caruso standing next to her. Rose bled in her periphery, taking in small sips of air. The stage was dark, as if night had fallen over all the world.

Tiber Caruso held out his hand. "Do you now see?"

She nodded. "I think I do, but I still don't understand."

He smiled. Ducked his head in agreement. "It was a long mystery. Time beyond counting, and the clues were difficult to follow. Hidden by the nature of those that sought their meaning."

Mickayla couldn't follow his words. His explanation seemed unreasonably complicated.

She looked down at Rose's calm face. The suffering only came to the surface of her features when she touched her. When she attempted to heal her. When she tried to use the spark for a purpose other than intended.

Other than that which was agreed upon so long ago on a lonely cliff overlooking the desert.

Mickayla reached for Tiber Caruso's hand, but she paused before making contact. "I don't regret healing the children."

He smiled and inclined his head. "Nor should you."

The spark expanded in anticipation.

She took the old man's hand. His fingers closed in hers in a desperate grip. He sighed in ecstasy, and the power left her without fanfare.

She pulled her hand back to find herself alone on the stage. No Rose. No table. Just shadows and drying blood.

She hung her head.

The oily trail still pulsed with movement. Like they were extensions of a larger animal under the floor. The appendages that breathed for whatever was seeking her out from the safe darkness.

As her attention fixed on the squirming mass, every end of the network trained in her direction. Flowed like water toward her where it all collected around her feet.

She was unable to register alarm. Just a partial curiosity.

Even when the squirming bugs poked through the surface. Collected into connected lines that stretched across the gap between her and the heaving oil slick, she only raised a single eyebrow.

Like blind maggots. Scanning the air as if to taste where she was.

A single stretching tentacle made contact with the hem of her jeans. The black fluid rolled along the scaffolding of the bugs that had reached her, and at the first contact, the rest of the roiling flow lifted up like the crest of a wave.

It crashed into her with the roar of plunging into a deep body of dark water. Rushing noise that allowed no thought. She tumbled into the burning flow. Rolled in the current. Sank to the bottom.

Her hands were pressed flat on the pier next to her thighs. She swung her feet over the edge where they splashed through the first couple of inches of cool Lake Winstead water.

She opened her eyes, and the clouds moved away from the sun. Her face was bathed in golden heat, and she smiled. Hummed a note of pleasure through her nose. Leaned back to tip her head up to the light.

Vibrations under her hands let her know somebody was coming. The rhythm of the gait was as familiar as her own. Her twin sister had stepped onto the dock.

She heard ice clink against the inside of a glass. Her smile became a grin as she anticipated what the beverage might be.

Rose padded to the end, where she dropped, folding into a cross-legged position. "Here you go, kid. Iced tea."

Mickayla cracked one eye open. "Does it have vodka in it?"

Rose shrugged. "Maybe."

Mickayla laughed as she took the offered glass. Took a sip, and it was cold and sweet, and there was plenty of vodka in it. She smacked her lips and sighed. "Perfect."

"I thought you might like it," Rose said.

Mickayla sidled over and held out her arm. Rose obliged by scooting into her embrace. Swinging her own legs over the edge.

Mickayla pulled her sister into her side. When she started crying, she shook her head in confusion. Rose glanced over with concern. "What's wrong, Mickey?"

Mickayla shrugged. "I just love you so much, you know? I'm just glad you're here."

Rose put her glass down. Reached up to grab Mickayla's hand dangling over her shoulder. "Stop being weird. I'm not going anywhere."

"I don't see how you could," Mickayla said. "I'm never letting you go."

Epilogue

CARL LEANED against the bar inside Reginald's Comedy Showcase. Even though it was a dump next to the Hyatt on 72nd street, it was a nice change of pace from the glitter-choking strippers and fish tacos of Hector's Basement. Paid better too.

He saw a lot of the same comics, though. Some of the jokes he could even recite by heart from hearing them so many times. He saw a lot of the same crowd too. Even though the Showcase pretended to be a higher label, it was the same generic rotation of amateurs trying to make it big, and the same kind of people came to watch.

Except tonight. The guy who had played the last twenty minutes was the real deal. Henry Black. Fat and bald and authentic. He had 'em eating out of his hand. Pissing themselves with laughter. *Choking* to death almost.

When Reggie came up to bring Henry back out on stage, Carl nearly choked *himself*. He'd never seen Reggie do that shit, and since Carl was bouncing past closing time, it put him into overtime, so he wasn't about to complain.

Besides ... lately ... he needed the distraction. Sleep

was hard to come by, and the only way he could take his mind off of it was punching drunks in the face. Going to the gym. Drinking too much.

He still didn't smoke, though.

Everybody had emptied out, and he was nursing the last of his warm beer. He'd get the bartender, Chet, to fill a growler that he'd knock back before going to bed tonight, but for now, he was still on the clock, so he had to stay sharp.

He looked back up at the stage and shook his head in amazement. Henry Black looked like he was about to score. Some dark-haired chick. Painfully hot.

He'd noticed her when she came in with her ID already showing. He'd swiped her through. Turned to watch her ass as she walked away. Forgot about her soon enough.

But there she was. Looking up at that fat and sweaty comedian with an expression that looked like worship. She must really like to laugh.

Henry was nervous. Bobbing his head. Wiping the sweat from his face and looking at the moisture in his hand. Carl wanted to go over there and tell the guy to calm the fuck down. Anybody barely looking could see she was into him.

He'd talked to Henry a couple of times back at Hector's. Liked the guy enough, just wasn't impressed by his presence. The chick obviously saw something *he* didn't.

He watched them talk as he finished his beer. Buttoned the top button of his shirt in preparation of the long walk to his car. Another El Camino. Not a '69, but it was a beautiful specimen, and it was delivered to his front door. Tags and titles ready to go.

Gift horses and all that.

Henry was still nodding like an idiot, but he and the

chick were headed Carl's way side-by-side. Henry's hand kept lifting up like it was gonna rest on her shoulder, only to fall back to his side like it thought better of it.

Carl shook his head. Looked down at his knuckles as they passed.

"So, what do you wanna do?" Henry asked.

"I don't know," the chick said. Her voice was sultry. Something to drive a man insane under the covers.

"How about doughnuts?" Henry said, with a little too much enthusiasm. "Or maybe Rocko's across the street?"

As she swung her jacket around to get it across her shoulders, Carl took a juke step and put his hip into her. She bounced away to fall toward Henry. The shocked comedian threw his arms open and caught her before she could fall.

Carl put his hands up, palms out. "My bad, bro!"

The chick giggled into Henry's chest, and when she stood back up, she had her arm around him. Henry's hand finally settled on her shoulder, and he looked at Carl over her head.

Carl winked. "*No hay bronca.* You kids have a good time."

The chick waved. Flashed him a grin full of perfect teeth. "Thanks."

He waved back and watched them leave hand-in-hand. Just before the door closed, Henry glanced back over his shoulder with a confused expression. It looked like it was gonna take a while for him to process what had just happened.

Carl didn't think Henry was stupid. After listening to his comedy, he was sure the guy was far from it. And even though it was often a comedian's job to be observant, he wasn't sure just how observant Henry really was when it came to women.

The door clicked shut, and Carl turned the deadbolt without ceremony. Turned to pick up the sealed jug of beer from the bar. Tipped Chet a salute as he walked to the back.

He had nothing invested in the relationship, but he sure hoped Henry scored with that chick tonight. Or *some* night. He shook his head in wonder. Maybe they'd even get married.

As he stepped into the alley to head toward the garage where he had parked to keep his car off the street, he nodded to himself. "Why not?"

Stranger things had happened. Many of them had even happened to *him*, so why not indeed?

He took a deep breath of the cool air. Summer was right around the corner. The heat would make the wharf down in Bay South stink something awful. Working this place was a pretty good gig. He might stick around until it started to get a little colder.

Bring the smell of the bay down a little. Maybe then he could go back to Hector's. It seemed like he was always crying anymore, but this time he let the tears flow.

He missed Mickayla so bad, and the water always made him think of her. He and Sister Wanda often talked about her. The old nun assured him that Mickayla had done a great service to the Lord, and though he believed her, he never accepted her offer to pray together.

He doubted if he'd ever pray again.

THE END...

THE CITIZENS of Burg City are blind. They can't even see when there's a monster among them. Henry Black was a successful standup comic who thought he finally had it all, until his family is murdered in front of him, and a deal with darkness itself, trading his soul for another shot at life and turning himself into the personification of twisted revenge. See how Henry fights the forces of darkness and the man who murdered his family in Soulless.

Click here to get Monstrous: The Complete Series

What to Read Next

If you loved reading *Soulless*, you should definitely go get *Monstrous* and start reading the *Monstrous* series today.

Get Monstrous Today

A Quick Favor

Thank you for reading *Soulless*.

If you enjoyed this book please consider writing a review of it on your favorite bookseller so other readers might enjoy it too. Just a couple of sentences. That would mean a lot to us.

Thank you!

About the Authors

Sawyer Black writes dark and violent fiction for people who secretly love puppies and rainbows. In addition to being a U.S. Army veteran, he's also a beardsman. In fact, that's where all his ideas come from. The beard. Speculative stories about struggle and triumph and brutal emotion, written mostly for his ideal reader, his wife of nearly twenty-five years. He's an independent woman who likes cigars and margaritas, and he holds the deep belief that the earth is round.

~

David W. Wright is the co-author of edge-of-your-seat thrillers including the best-selling post-apocalyptic series *Yesterday's Gone*, the paranoid sci-fi *WhiteSpace* series, and the vigilante series, *No Justice*, as well as standalone thrillers *12*, and *Crash* which was recently optioned for a movie.

David is an accomplished, though intermittent, cartoonist who lives in [LOCATION REDACTED] with his wife and son [NAMES REDACTED.]

He is not at all paranoid.

He is "the grumpy one" on *The Story Studio Podcast* with fellow Sterling and Stone founders, Sean Platt and Johnny B. Truant.

You can email him at david@sterlingandstone.net

We swear, he almost never bites. Unless you feed him after midnight.

~

For any questions about Sterling & Stone books or products, or help with anything at all, please send an email to help@sterlingandstone.net, or contact us at sterlingand stone.net/contact. Thank you for reading.

Also By David W. Wright

Cold Vengeance

Cold Vengeance

Cold Reckoning

Hidden Justice

Hidden Justice

Hidden Honor

Hidden Shame

Hidden Virtue

No Justice

No Justice

No Escape

No Hope

No Return

No Stopping

No Fear

Karma Police

Jumper

Karma Police

The Collectors

Deviant

The Fall

Homecoming

Yesterday's Gone

October's Gone

Yesterday's Gone Season One

Yesterday's Gone Season Two

Yesterday's Gone Season Three

Yesterday's Gone Season Four

Yesterday's Gone Season Five

Yesterday's Gone Season Six

Tomorrow's Gone

Tomorrow's Gone Season One

Tomorrow's Gone Season Two

Tomorrow's Gone Season Three

Available Darkness

Darkness Itself

Available Darkness Book One

Available Darkness Book Two

Available Darkness Book Three

WhiteSpace

WhiteSpace Season One

WhiteSpace Season Two

WhiteSpace Season Three

Stand Alone Novels

Crash

Emily's List

Threshold

The Secret Within